THE INNOCENCE OF DEATH

ON BEHALF OF DEATH, BOOK I

E.G STONE

TARNEY BRAE CREATIVE ENDEAVOURS

Copyright © 2021 by E.G Stone

A Tarney Brae Creative Endeavours Production

Cover design by Fae Lane

Editing by Michael Evan

ISBN 978-1-7347965-6-8

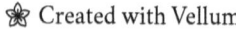 Created with Vellum

For D, in thanks for the lasagna

CONTENTS

THE INSTANT OF DEATH

*H*ave you ever had a time where you thought things were going really, really well and life could hardly be better? Have you walked around with a smile on your face, knowing precisely where things are going to end up? The world is about to be laid at your feet. Everything is good. Fantastic, even. That's usually right about the time when Life likes to kick you in the shins, let me tell you.

I've met Life. She delights in being unfair and favours only those who fight her. Death, on the other hand is far more of a gentleman, if slightly scarier... well, perhaps I'd better start at the beginning.

My name is Cal Thorpe. Of Harcourt Marketing? I was their top marketing manager and public relations agent, well on my way up the ladder. I had been in this job about four years, and I was doing good. No, not good. Spectacular. I had just finished up a highly-successful marketing campaign for a sports medicine doctor who had written a book about some journey in some foreign country where he discovered the secret to life or some such nonsense. It was an overdone idea, but I had marketed it and done fantastically well. The sales had hit the New York Times bestseller list in a week, and his social media following was enormous. He had talks scheduled with all the national shows and there were even whispers of an international tour. I was just that good.

Anyways, on this particular night, I was walking through the park on a shortcut to a celebratory dinner, likely to do with my recent success. Old lady Harcourt —the widow of the original owner—was being generous enough to treat me and a few of the other executives at a steak house across the city. Ostensibly, the dinner was to celebrate the firm's mention in one of the top business associations, but I think everyone in attendance really knew what was going on. When you got in with her, you were *in*. I could see a vice presidency in my near future.

Basically, things were going well for me. Really well. I was making money faster than I could spend it. I was practically rolling in new clients. Even now, my phone was vibrating with requests from people to take them on. My assistant had stepped in months ago to field most of those, but even the ones that went through kept me busy at all hours. I had a fancy apartment that had more space than your average big-city digs and a view that photographers would envy. Not that I actually needed the space, since I didn't have a girlfriend or even a cat, but it was worth every penny. I wore tailored suits. Patent leather shoes. Had designer glasses. My social media pages were growing exponentially, and I was about to have dinner with someone who thought her diamond bracelet was casual wear.

I was on top of the world.

And then, I wasn't.

"Give me your wallet." A pressure in my side.

I panicked.

There was a man mugging me in the middle of the park. He had a gun. "Give it to me!"

"A-alright," I said, holding up my hands. All the success in the world couldn't stop them from shaking. I reached into my jacket pocket and tried not to pass out.

"No funny business," the man growled, pressing his gun deeper into my side.

"N-no o-o-of course n-not," I stammered. I was reaching into my pocket when a dog barked from not far away. My mugger cursed violently and jerked against me. I felt time slow down. My heart beat once in my ears, blocking out all noise. For that fleeting moment, I was certain everything would be alright. The mugger would run. I would call the police. Go to dinner. Then, there was a spectacular roaring clap and I was even more certain that I was going to die.

"Good evening, Mr. Thorpe."

I gaped at the figure in the three-piece suit. He had a hat on—one of those wool fedoras from the 1940s— and it shaded most of his features. All I could see was that he was tall, slim, dressed in clothes that cost more than my last pay check—a three-piece suit with an embroidered silk waistcoat that matched his bright red pocket square—and that he was floating two inches above the ground. Oh, and he hadn't been there two seconds before.

"I'm dead," I said stupidly.

"No, not yet," the figure said, striding casually forwards. His feet touched lightly on the ground as he moved towards me, like he was fully appearing in this time and this place. His hands were in his pockets, completely relaxed and at ease. Didn't he realise that there was a man with a gun right here? That I had been shot?

"I've been shot!" I'm fairly certain my intelligence had flown out the window. Apparently I didn't do well in life-or-death situations.

"No, not yet. You are *about* to be shot. There is a difference." His voice was kind and gentle, not at all judgemental, despite my panic and incoherence. "Look. See."

I jumped away from my attacker and stared, mouth open like an idiot. The mugger—hood up, jeans torn, gun shining—was perfectly still, desperation twisting his features. Where I had been standing, was a single piece of metal. A bullet, suspended in mid-air, not moving. Had it continued on its path, I would most certainly be dead.

But I wasn't.

"Am I hallucinating?" I asked carefully.

"That depends," the figure said, shrugging. "How creative are you?"

"Uh-huh. I'm lying on the ground, bleeding out and this is what my brain comes up with to make it all better." I patted myself down desperately, afraid that I was going to feel blood. Afraid that I wasn't.

"If you like. How about we go sit on that bench and have a talk." He nodded to a spot not a hundred feet away, pleasantly lit by the street lights along the path. There were even flowers growing by the bench. "This might make things clearer."

"Alright," I agreed. It wasn't as though I had much else better to do. I was never going to make my dinner, now. I was going to give up everything I had worked to achieve, by missing this dinner, by being almost shot in the park. Somehow, I doubted that the old bat would take dying as an excuse. Oddly enough, though, I didn't really mind.

We sat on the bench. The light from the lamp post filtered down so that my companion's face was still completely in shadow. I could see his hands though. They were long, elegant and blacker than charcoal. It seemed an unnatural colour, not quite human. I knew and was friends with plenty of black men and women and had never seen someone whose skin seemed to just absorb light.

"I have come to offer you a job," the figure said. He brushed some dust from his knee. I blinked.

"Really? My hallucination offers me a job?"

"I would like you to be my publicist or marketing

specialist or whatever the term is." He ignored my dig about being a hallucination. I wasn't sure what that meant.

"You want me to be your PR guy?" I scuffed my shoe over the concrete, flattening a few blades of grass that managed to spring through the tough material. "Are you having image problems? Bad publicity can kill a career, you know."

"Oh, I am well aware." I got the impression that he was smiling. I wanted to see his face, but the part of me that had learned good manners—some clients would bite your head off for asking anything remotely personal—wouldn't ask. So I just nodded blithely.

"You sure picked a bad time to ask me to represent you." I jerked my head back to where the mugger stood, frozen. Maybe my good manners weren't all that well developed, after all.

"It was the only time I *could* ask you, I'm afraid. I am bound by certain rules. But here, in my domain, I can do as I wish," the figure said. I frowned. His domain? I was beginning to think that I wasn't hallucinating. I wasn't nearly this creative. I had failed my creative writing course during my undergraduate degree, with a note from the professor stating *'this is impressively terrible'* on the final exam. It was supposed to be impossible to fail that course.

"Who are you?" I asked, a bit rudely.

"You don't want to guess? I think you could come up with some very interesting answers. No? Very well." He reached up with those long fingers and removed his hat. Some part of my mind started screaming, but I was too well trained in image preservation to do more than raise my eyebrows in surprise. Though, I fear I did whimper.

Like his hands, his skin was blacker than black. Shadows seemed to wreath around him, keeping the light away. His face was thin, gaunt almost, and he had a pleasant smile, though his teeth were not showing. He had no hair, no eyebrows or beard or anything. But that wasn't the most startling thing. No, it was the fact that he had no eyes. Not just skin where eyes should be, not lids closed permanently shut, but empty sockets. The darkness was vast in those two holes, and if I stared far enough for long enough, I would probably start seeing the end of the world. As it was, I saw my own life flash before my eyes. Several times. It was the same all the way through, except it ended in several different ways, all gruesomely laid out before me.

Shot.

Diseased.

Car Accident.

Drunk.

Drugs.

Violent murder.

Suicide by jumping.

Drowning.

I gasped and forced myself to blink, breaking whatever hold this thing had on me. I put my head between my knees and tried hard not to vomit. After a moment, I sat back up, my mouth dry. My terrifying companion just raised his brows, an unusual expression from what was basically a skin-covered skull. "Do you understand, now?" he asked kindly.

"Why don't you spell it out for me," I rasped, my heart racing. There was no doubt in my mind that I was not lying on the ground bleeding out after being mugged. Whatever this was, it was horrific and far too real.

"I am Death," he said gently.

"Ah," I said. I fought the urge to put my head back between my knees and breathe slowly. Instead, I clenched my hands into fists on my knees. "I see."

"Do you? So many have a difficult time accepting this," Death replied, obviously pleased. I swallowed down another whimper.

"I can't believe I'm sitting here with Death. And that you're offering me a job. Aren't you supposed to, well, I don't know what, actually. I can't believe this. I can't," I muttered. I could believe it, actually. Despite living a perfectly normal life up until this moment, disbelieving things like Bigfoot and the Loch Ness monster, I found I could believe this. I just didn't want to.

"Yes, now you see my problem. Why I want to hire you?" Death folded his hands neatly in his lap.

"You definitely need a PR specialist," I agreed. My heart was racing, I was probably seconds away from passing out, and I was talking calmly with Death about marketing. Maybe being shot was the better option. "I...I can't just take you on as a client through Harcourt, you know."

"Of course not. Your world is not ready for such things," Death scoffed, brushing his fingers over his hat. "No, you would have to come with me. You will be well compensated. I can offer you a place to live, staff, resources, whatever you need."

I was quiet for a moment, running the implications through my mind. Work for Death. And not through normal means. I would have to *go* with *Death*.

"I'd have to leave here, wouldn't I?" I said. "I couldn't just...freelance for you?"

"Unfortunately, that is not how this works." Death's voice grew colder. He nodded over to the frozen mugger. "I stopped you in the Instant of Death. I have only two options. Either I take you into my employ, which means that you are bound to me and my realm, or I return you to die. That is how this works. That is all I can offer."

I swallowed, feeling a pain in my chest. "I'd never get to come back here?"

"Not as you were. I could, occasionally, allow you back under a special dispensation, but you would not be as you are now."

"Why not?" Great plan, Cal. Ask stupid questions. If I go with Death, of course I wouldn't be the same. Well, I could hope, couldn't I? I was still young and invincible, wasn't I?

"Because I will have removed you from the fate of the mortal realms, the world here. I could not simply let you return, to play havoc with the fate of the future.

You would be separate, removed. And that requires certain changes."

I swallowed again, leaning back against the bench and looking at the sky. There were no stars. It was just shadow, reflecting the lights of the city. It might be my last time looking at the sky, and there weren't even stars to look at. "I don't want to die."

"Not many do."

"I mean, I've just gotten to the good part of my life. I'm doing well. I'm a success! I have a purpose and a reason to get up in the morning," I pleaded. Death looked at me and I suddenly felt very, very small. Okay, sure I wasn't as tall as he was. I was an average person, with an average life and average looks. My hair was even an average shade of brown and I wore glasses. But it was *my* average life. I was doing well at it. No, not well. Spectacular. I didn't want to give it up.

"You would still have a life," Death pointed out. "You would still be marketing, still have a purpose. It would just be in a different place. With wonders to occupy your every moment. And magic most people never even dream about."

"But I would have to give up everything I have here," I said.

"Yes," Death nodded. He paused, then, "Well, not everything. I could let you take your belongings with you."

"But everything else. Friends. Family. All gone."

"Yes," Death nodded again, still infuriatingly calm. "Though it does not much matter, really. Your choice is not between a life working for me and a life working for Harcourt. Your choice is between life and death, as it were. No pun intended."

"Mmmm," I smiled weakly. I took a deep breath and tried to be reasonable. Think logically. My options were death or Death. Obviously, there wasn't much of a choice. "Alright," I said. "But I have to tell you, there are a few things we need to agree on. First, I'm your PR agent and marketing specialist. All your decisions that might be seen by anybody and analysed or criticised or even noticed, you run through me. I'll be needing as much information as possible about your activities. That way, I can make sure they're painted in a good light...Do you have social media wherever it is we're going?"

"Indeed," Death said, frowning. "It is a pervasive thing to spread so far from this realm."

"Good. I'll get started on your accounts first thing."

"So you agree?"

"Didn't I just say I agreed?" I snapped. Snapping at your new boss, Death or not, is probably never a good idea. In my defence, I was having a bad day. He did not seem to mind, though, as he just sat there as calm and cool as ever. I shivered.

"Very well," Death smiled again. "Then I insist we shake hands."

He held out his shadowy appendage and I could feel the raw power coming off of his skin. I coughed nervously. "Is that strictly necessary?"

"Actually, yes," Death said. "It binds you to me and seals the contract. It will not kill you."

"Ha ha," I replied drily. I took his hand.

Power flooded through me, touching every nerve ending I had and setting each and every one of them on fire. I was pretty sure I screamed, but my brain was too overwhelmed by whatever was happening to take note. I saw colours swirling around me that didn't exist in nature. There were sounds running through my head, somewhere between a scream and a song. I could see Death, as calm as ever, sitting there, looking not at all regretful about what was happening. The corners of his mouth twitched in a smile.

Then, I passed out.

DEATH WARMED OVER

When I woke up, everything hurt. Not in the, "oh, let me take stock of what is still functioning after I ran that 10k yesterday" way. No, everything *hurt*, in the "I think I'm going to die and I can't tell anyone because I can't breathe and the phone is across the room" way. My limbs were on fire and there was some sort of pointed hammer pounding in my head. A weight lay on my chest and I was fairly certain I couldn't move my toes.

Somehow, I managed to exhale and let out a low whimper. That made everything hurt more.

A figure appeared in my line of sight and I realised that I could, actually, see. The figure slipped my glasses on my nose and the world became clearer. Everything was white. Startlingly white, like a brand new hospital with all the lights turned on. Except for the figure staring down at me, which made it all the more terrifying. It was small and misshapen. Its head resembled a squat pumpkin, except it was a strange shade of green. Its eyes were bright yellow bulbs with slits like a goat and its ears pointed outwards from its head like some sort of weird elf.

"Ah, you are awake," it rasped in a strange voice with an even stranger accent, like it had swallowed a Russian dictionary in Jamaica. It showed an unhealthy number of pointed teeth. I whimpered again and somehow managed to avoid a new wave of excruciating pain. "And you made the transition surprisingly well! Not many humans can stand to have their life-force ripped from them."

"Urghlgrlgl?" I tried to ask.

The creature spread its lips in a grin, showing even more teeth.

"Yes, you are doing very well indeed! Most would not be able to speak for days." The creature moved out of my line of sight. No matter how I tried, I couldn't move my head to follow it, so I listened. There was clinking, scraping over wood. I thought I heard the sound of claws at one point. None of this, whatever it was, made me feel any better. In fact, I'm fairly certain I was about to be drawn into the throes of a panic attack. If I could move to have a panic attack, that was.

The creature appeared again, this time much closer than it had been. I screamed—or groaned, which in my state was much the same thing—and the creature grinned wider. "Now, now, none of that. You're in good hands, you are. Old Doctor Graveltoes will take care of you. Best in Elsewhere, that's right!"

Nothing in that speech made any sense to me. I opened my mouth to protest louder and hopefully draw someone else's attention. The moment I did, this Graveltoes thing poured a warm liquid down my throat. It tasted of dirt and spoiled potatoes. I gagged, but considering I was completely prone, had no choice but to swallow it or suffocate.

The effect was immediate. The tingling in my limbs lessened and my headache felt less like a hammer and more like a tiny needle. I felt that I could actually move my joints, though not far. The world suddenly seemed clearer.

Which was about the point that I remembered just what I had done to bring me here.

I had made a deal with Death.

I couldn't go back to my life. Everything I knew was gone. I was way, way out of my element.

I opened my mouth to scream again, but Graveltoes put a hand over my mouth. Its skin was slick and cold.

"Yes, your understanding returns." Graveltoes nodded sagely. I turned my head to look fully at the spindly creature and it nodded. "Good, good. Another dose in an hour, and you'll be right as rain. The Master wants to see you. Sent me in to make certain you were fit for visiting."

I struggled to sit up and take some control of the situation. Graveltoes clucked like an old woman and helped me. "Where…?" was about all I could manage.

"Give it time, human," the creature said, rolling its bulbous eyes with impatience. "Always rushing about. You'd think you were going to die at any moment."

Graveltoes started laughing violently and had to go support itself by the white wall to keep from falling over. I frowned, wanting to roll my eyes myself. My head still hurt too much for that. Thankfully, we were interrupted before the creature could make any more terrible jokes, or pour any more foul liquid down my throat.

The door—one I hadn't noticed before on the opposite wall—opened, letting Death in. Maybe it was because the room was so white, or because we were in Death's realm—so I presumed, at least—but his skin seemed blacker than usual. Though, I didn't tremble in fear, so at least we were making progress. Shadows wreathed themselves around him and trailed behind him. He still wore the immaculate three-piece suit. This time, though, I noticed the Italian leather shoes and the neat red trim at the cuffs of his jacket. Death, believe it or not, was a dandy.

"You are recovering. Good," he said, striding into the room.

Graveltoes grovelled at Death's feet, twisting his shoulders while looking at Death in some sort of strange, twisted bow. "I have given the human the draught. He improves."

"Good. You may go," Death waved a hand. Graveltoes bowed deeper and slipped out of the room, closing the door. It was probably a sign of my mental disturbance that I found being alone with Death more comforting than being with that gremlin-goblin creature thing, doctor or not.

Death pulled a chair up and sat beside the bed. I was fairly certain the chair hadn't been there before, but I wasn't going to say anything. Not that I *could* say anything. My throat continued to remain closed.

"I trust you are improving?" Death said, as though he didn't know. I worked my jaw and swallowed, trying to make my voice work.

"What… happened?" I staggered out, my voice sounding rough even to my own ears. I really wanted some water, but there was none in sight. Only more of that dreadful liquid, which I hoped never to taste again.

"I stripped you of your life-force, replacing it with my own power. You had to be bound to me in order to enter my domain without issue. Most immortals would have few problems, but humans are notoriously fragile."

I glared. He could have warned me.

"If I had warned you, it would not have made things any more pleasant," Death said with a casual shrug. Great, now he was a mind reader. "You made the deal willingly. That will lessen the aftereffects greatly. Another few hours and you should be able to walk around. I will send someone to fetch you and bring you to my realm, then."

"Am I…dead?" I managed. Death smiled and shook his head, the shadows moving with him.

"You are not dead, per se. Neither are you alive. You

have, essentially, become an immortal without having the usual magic in your blood. Were I a master of Time, then you would be simply...stuck. As it is, you simply *are*. No more, no less." Death waved his long fingers and I felt the last traces of my former self quaver.

I wasn't dead. I wasn't alive. Did that mean I couldn't die, either? Would I age? No, it sounded like I was going to remain precisely as I was, in the prime of my, well, life. That was, in some sense, very cool. It was what so many people dreamed of. What doctors worked endlessly for. But it was also the only part of my life I still had. I couldn't visit my friends, my family, any of it. They would all think I was dead—or worse, that I might never have existed. And now my humanity was being taken from me, too.

I clenched my jaw. No. I might not be mortal anymore, but I was still human. I *had* to be. Right?

"I can see the implications of our deal were not quite fully realised upon sealing," Death said, turning his vacant eyes on me. "There will be a period of adjustment, I would imagine."

"Where...are we?" My voice was slightly clearer. My mind, though, refused to dwell on the metaphysical realities of my new existence. It was far easier to focus on the mundane, such as where I was, or what that *thing* Graveltoes was.

"This room is part of the hospital. Doctor Gravel-toes oversees the patients. Given that he mostly has to deal with such creatures as do not get sick or die except by some extreme circumstance, he was quite eager to meet you," Death said. "Doctors are, as you might expect, not terribly common amongst the immortal or the magical."

I waited, not encouraged that I was a source of curiosity to Graveltoes.

"As to the rest, we are in Elsewhere."

"Sorry?" I coughed. Death waved his hand and a glass of water—with a re-useable straw, even— appeared. I took it eagerly, doing my best to ignore the strain as I moved.

"Elsewhere. It is the land of the immortals—as opposed to the mortal realms, where I found you—a land of magic and everything that humanity has forgotten. Some call it Avalon, some call it the spirit world, but it is all the same place. It touches the mortal realms in significant points in time and space. Some of it exists tangentially to your own world, some does not. You will find many familiar things here—like your social media—and many more unfamiliar. My realm occupies but a small portion of Elsewhere."

"But you're Death," I said, sipping more water. "Shouldn't you control all the souls? Like the Under-world or the afterlife or whatever?"

Death threw back his head and laughed. The sound was highly unusual, like receiving an electric shock. All the hair on my body stood on end and I was fairly certain that my heart stopped for a moment. It wasn't beautiful. Nor did it fill me with a feeling of joy or pleasure or elation. It was, frankly, mildly terrifying.

"My dear human," Death grinned, pulling a finger

under his empty eye socket as though he were wiping away tears. "I am not responsible for the souls of those who die! I cause death. I am called a ferryman, though even that is not accurate. I am a transition, a state of being, an event. What happens afterwards is something far more complex and personal and powerful. Even I am not privy to the mysteries of that!"

He chuckled for a moment longer and I tried to force my heart rate down. This job was going to be a lot more complicated than I thought.

"I'm sure you have more questions, but I have duties to attend to," Death flicked his wrist, almost like checking a watch. He wasn't wearing a watch. "I will send your assistant to you and she can get you acquainted with your duties and the Elsewhere. I will have transportation sent once Doctor Graveltoes decides you are fit. We will have time later to discuss things more thoroughly."

"Uh...okay," I said, suddenly feeling very tired. The glass of water I was holding vanished, as did the chair Death was sitting on. Death strode to the door in his strange, graceful glide. He didn't turn back as he left. I wasn't sure I wanted him to do so.

—

I woke some time later with the uncomfortable feeling that I was being watched. I opened my eyes and adjusted my glasses, blinking to clear the blurriness away. I yelped.

Sure enough, I *was* being watched. Closely.

This creature was built along the lines of an American football running-back: massive shoulders, thick neck, a head that could probably go through a brick wall. The creature's skin was a deep grey colour, pebbled with what looked like beads that made a shimmering effect under the white light. It was completely bald and had oversized, twisted features. A squashed nose, blinking great eyes reflecting bright greenish-yellow, a brow line that would have looked suitable on a sculpture of early humans. I saw all of this in great detail, but could see no more of the creature because it was leaning disturbingly close to my bed. And my face.

After I jerked away with my yelp, the creature straightened and grinned, revealing an incongruous set of perfectly straight and slightly blinding teeth. "Ah, you are awake! I wasn't sure how long you would sleep. How long do humans normally sleep?"

"Er, about eight hours a night," I replied, completely flummoxed. Honestly, how *do* you reply differently to that question. "Sorry, who are you?"

"I am Yolanda. Your assistant. Death assigned me to help you," the creature said, nodding firmly. I took another look and sure enough, this creature was built along the lines of a female. A massive one. Who could probably squish me like a bug. I closed my eyes and swallowed, taking a moment.

I looked at Yolanda again. "Sorry…I don't mean to be rude, but *what* are you?"

Yolanda laughed, the sound nothing like Death's

laugh. It was loud, boisterous, a bit deep, and remarkably human. There was some relief in that. "You are not rude, human, you are ignorant! There is a difference. I am a troll."

"A troll," I repeated somewhat weakly. Death was one thing. A troll? Something else entirely.

"*Rock* troll. Not like those cave trolls. They're nasty, they are. They think anything that walks above ground is a waste of space. And they're mean when they can't find enough food." Yolanda rolled her eyes. My goodness, she sounded almost exactly like my old assistant Rachel. The same gossipy conversation, the same amount of over information. It was so *bizarre*.

"Right," I tried to smile, but it was about as weak as my voice. "Um, I'm Cal. It's good to meet you."

Yolanda took my hand and shook it firmly, which felt like all my bones were being squished together. "You think I'm ugly and scary. Most humans do. But you will learn. There are things that are far more dangerous than a troll. And I'm a good worker. I know all about computers. Python, Java, web design, all of it. I even hacked into the vampire wifi once, just to see if I could."

I let out a chuckle, surprised by the honesty of the sound. "Yolanda, I think we'll get on just fine."

She beamed at me.

Graveltoes approved me for getting on with my new job about ten minutes after Yolanda woke me up. I swallowed down another of those vial draughts and my headache was nearly gone. Yolanda helped me out of bed and we tottered out of the white room and into a building that looked much the same as any human hospital, minus the patients. Also, there were shields splattered in blood on the walls. About the time we reached the sliding doors, I was walking steadily, if slowly, on my own. Yolanda pointed eagerly down to the street, where Death said his transportation would meet us.

I had sort of expected a ghostly carriage with spectral horses, perhaps with fire coming out of their noses or their skeletons showing through. If not that, then maybe a hearse, driven by a solemn and probably dead chauffeur. What I did not expect was a 1920s style Rolls Royce Phantom, with a lean looking chauffeur leaning against it. This chauffeur looked perfectly normal: black suit, shoes, human face and body.

Maybe it was that one instance of normality, but I nearly sagged to the ground in relief. I wasn't in a world surrounded by monsters and inhuman things that I had no name for. I was in a place that was different—wildly so—but still had things like cars and perfectly normal chauffeurs. For all I knew, he was another human like me, dragged to this world at the Instant of Death.

Then, the chauffeur lifted his head and I saw his eyes. Empty with twin blue flames where the eyes should be. It wasn't like Death, where the emptiness held power and vast amounts of it. They weren't even truly empty sockets. There was just fire where the eyes should be. And it was with hunger that the chauffeur looked at Yolanda and myself.

I let out a whimper, barely audible, as we slid into the back seat of the car. At least, I thought it was barely audible. The chauffeur lifted his eyebrows in surprise and loomed over the door. Yolanda just shrugged her massive shoulders, patting me on the leg. "He's human. New to Elsewhere. Doesn't know a troll from a goblin."

"I see," the chauffeur said. His voice was like ice, sending a shiver up my spine. I took a deep breath. I had to be polite. I had to win these people over. How could I be a good marketing agent if I couldn't even do that? That was my job, now. My purpose. My only tie to everything I had left behind.

And I failed miserably. I couldn't manage a smile or a polite nod of the head. All I managed to do was stare, wide-eyed, at my hands. I could barely control the trembling. The chauffeur, thank goodness, didn't seem bothered by this. He just closed the door and walked around to the front of the car.

"Wraiths are always a bit difficult," Yolanda said, patting me on the knee again. "They have such a hard time controlling their hunger."

"Hunger for what?" My voice came out as a squeak.

"Life," she said with a shrug. "That's why they work for Death. No one else would have them. But they're not all bad. Yggdral there is one of the nicest I know. Well, except for that lapse on Christmas. The staff was never quite the same after that."

I was silent. What could I say to *that*? I was trembling in my shoes and I had absolutely no idea what I was doing. Only thing was, I had to figure it out quickly or things were going to end very badly indeed for the late Cal Thorpe. I had to get a grip on myself. This was all insane—there was no doubt—but it was also my new existence. I had been brought here for a particular purpose, and right now I was letting myself down. I needed to adapt. Quickly. What happened if I accidentally offended someone because I didn't know what was going on? Would that offence result in my actual death? Could Death even stop that? If I were so stupid as to do something like that, I wasn't certain Death would bother to stop it.

"Yolanda," I said slowly, looking up from my hands about ten minutes into the drive, once I managed to get some deep breathing in. "Is there some sort of guide I can read to Elsewhere?"

Yolanda tilted her head. "No one's ever bothered to write it down. Or been allowed to. Lots of races have their little secrets, you know, and they don't like others knowing about it. Take us rock trolls. I don't mind telling you, because you wouldn't use it against us, right?"

"No, of course not!" I widened my eyes to reassure her. As far as I was concerned, trolls were about the nicest people I had met so far.

Yolanda smiled, revealing those strangely straight teeth again. "Well, rock trolls love salt. Salty food, that is. The crystals are useless when they're not in food.

Not even very pretty to look at. You can get some of us to do almost anything for salty food."

"Like popcorn?" I tried cracking a smile. I don't think it broke my face or anything.

"Exactly like popcorn," Yolanda said with a fluttery sigh. "But they don't make it very well here. So many things *hate* salt in Elsewhere. So we have to sneak over to the mortal realms and steal as much as we can. We get into a lot of trouble that way."

"Trouble? Like with the humans seeing you or something? Surely they couldn't hurt you," I laughed weakly. Yolanda took the joke and laughed louder, the sound shaking the car. The wraith in the front seat cast a glance over his shoulder. I couldn't quite tell if he was amused; the fire leaping from his eyes didn't really make reading him easy.

"Humans hurt a troll?! Ha! You are so funny!" She shook her massive shoulders and threw her head back. "No, we have to look out for the Guardians. They keep the Elsewhere separate. They're like your, ah...dentists? People who arrest you and lock you up?"

"Police," I corrected. It occurred to me, with that small lapse, that I had no idea how all these creatures knew English. Or so much about the human world. The vocabulary. Heck, even the technology in the hospital had looked relatively human. Not to mention we were driving in an honest to goodness car. If the Elsewhere had Guardians to keep people separate, surely they didn't cross over much, did they?

"Right, police," Yolanda nodded. "Anyways, the

Guardians keep things separate. They have a pretty good grip on things. Of course, there are places where they have no authority at all. The ones whose magic is still connected to the mortal realms, for one. Or whose magic is old enough to stretch back before the split between the realms. There aren't many of those about anymore."

"Er, does *everyone* have magic here?" I asked, alarmed. How was I meant to defend myself against a world of magic?

"No," Yolanda snorted. The normally chatty troll kept quiet long enough to tell me that was the end of *that* conversation. I thought about pressing the issue—it seemed rather relevant to my survival—but I didn't want to alienate the one person who was actively helping me. Instead, I busied myself with looking out the window.

I nearly threw myself back into a state of panic.

It was almost like the real world. The mortal realms, I mean. There were trees and plants and walls and roads and even buildings that looked vaguely familiar. But it was so much more, too. The trees were taller and seemed more aware than anything I had ever come across. The plants were vibrant colours that never existed in nature. The buildings were all from a world that was hundreds of years gone. They looked like a reconstruction of a medieval period, but everything was in perfect order and I doubted had ever been subject to the ravages of time.

We were moving too fast to see any real detail, but I

did see a massive shape off in the distance that could have been a dragon. There were shapes that looked like people, but with wings stretching behind them, or curling horns sprouting out of their heads. Some shapes didn't look like people at all, but more like Yolanda or Graveltoes. There were things walking on four legs that looked like no animal I had ever seen. I wanted to take it all in, to ask questions about everything. We kept driving, though.

For the rest of the drive, I had my nose pressed to the window. Maybe I was still hallucinating. Maybe I was in a hospital in a coma and would never wake up. Maybe all of this was real. But whatever it was, it was *amazing*.

"Is everything like this in Elsewhere?" I asked as we turned off the main road.

Yolanda looked out the window and gave a casual 'huh'. "Not everywhere. Some places are much nicer. There's the Icelands, of course, for beings of Winter. And there's the Lakes, for the water creatures. I like Death's lands, myself, but I'm biased."

I was about to ask what Death's lands were like, but I saw for myself. It was as if we had suddenly leaped from one place to the next. The colours shifted, changed to a more silver and grey and blue spectrum. There were still plants and trees, but it was as if they were magnificent ghosts of the things. Yet they were still possessed of a certain vitality, pulsating with a shadowy power. I did not see any houses along the road. There were no creatures moving about, no animals, no sign of civilisation at all. Like the lands were holding their breath.

Beautiful, yes. But deadly and haunting.

"The Lands of Silence," Yolanda sighed, like a weary traveller returning home. "Welcome to your new home, Cal."

This was going to take some getting used to.

DEATH AT THE OFFICE

The rest of my day and the next one after that seemed completely normal by comparison. Well, when I say completely normal, I mean in the sense that if such a thing had happened to me back in the mortal realms, I would have thought I won the lottery. Why? Because I was shown where I would live and work. I was shown to the door of a very large house that held my living space and my offices. There was even a sign outside the door: Cal Thorpe Marketing. If I hadn't been freaked out at the whole situation, I would have been frozen in shock.

The house itself was far larger than anything I could have even considered affording in the city. It was done in the imposing Victorian-gothic style, with stones, slate roof, carved reliefs (oddly, these were of humans rather than gargoyles) and crawling ivy to match. Only, the ivy was a silvery grey, the reliefs all showed images of people dying and the house looked like it had never been lived in before. To be honest, it was not really my style, being a bit too looming and obviously magical. I was now working for Death, though. It seemed fitting.

At least the interior was modern.

The inside was split into two separate sections. The front of the house held my offices. They were done in the most modern minimalist fashion, with greys and whites everywhere, the furniture of black leather, the decorations of steel and glass. My desk, though, was curiously old fashioned: heavy, solid wood with hand-carved detail and drawers that locked with skeleton keys. I had all the newest computers to play with and Yolanda fairly squealed over her alcove and desk, set slightly away from the reception area.

The living space was a study in contrast to the office. Where the office had been modern, the living space was old fashioned. Dark, heavy colours, swooping bookshelves, wooden furniture that one person couldn't lift on their own. It was a little oppressive, to be honest. It needed a bit of colour, maybe even a steampunk motif. Thank goodness, though, someone had thought ahead about plumbing, heating, cooling and every other modern convenience.

The weird part was that all of my belongings from my apartment back in the real world were there. They had been unpacked and put away exactly as I would have done, down to the towels in the linen closet. There was even human food in the kitchen—all the best products, except for the overabundance of salted snacks. Yolanda helped me sort those out.

After a day of puttering around, exploring the area and seeing where, exactly, my toothbrush had been stowed, I was permanently wearing a confused and stunned expression. I shuffled into my office, wearing slacks and a sweater that had been brought over and put in my closet.

"You look funny," Yolanda said, swivelling in the oversized office chair behind her desk.

"Do I?"

Yolanda nodded. "Yes. Are we going to start working, now?"

I looked around. This was the whole point of my being here. To work. To market Death. I could stall by doing research on Elsewhere, about the creatures I was likely to interact with, but that would be denying the obvious. My life had changed. I didn't even recognise myself in the mirror. It was time to get over that and start doing what I did best.

"Alright," I said, cleaning my glasses on the edge of my sweater. "I want you to set up social media accounts. Pinterest, Instagram, Twitter, Tumblr. Not Facebook. They've had enough problems recently without adding Death to the mix. Are there any others you can think of?"

"WhoWhere," Yolanda said. I blinked. "It's an Elsewhere-specific service. Like The Book Face and that one a few years ago…"

"Myspace? LinkedIn?" I asked.

"Google!" Yolanda grinned. I struggled to wrap my mind around the two concepts merging into one and failed. "I will set them all up."

"Um...great. Do we have access to pictures? For the profiles. And I'd like to get following some of his friends or associates before we do any posting. Is there anyone I can interview that has worked closely with Death? Or friends? I'd like to get a sense of him and what he does. How he interacts with people. I need a strategy and I need a sense of Death to work out what I need to do."

Yolanda screwed up her face in thought. "I do not know his friends. I do not interact with him, only work for him."

I scowled. "There has to be *somebody*. Marketing campaigns are personal things. I'm selling a person, dealing with his public appearances, online interactions, making sure people *like* him. Or, well...want to work with him, or recognise him. He said he needed image help. But why? What have people been saying about him?"

Yolanda shrugged, looking a bit wary. "There are a couple of associates I could, ah, call in..."

"Do it," I nodded. She blinked and hunched her shoulders, but nodded, turning to the computer and smart phone on her desk. I left her to it and went to my own desk, pulling up the same social media sites I had mentioned to Yolanda. My old life didn't exist anymore, so I needed to start from scratch. And no good marketing agent didn't market himself.

I spent the next two hours figuring out my social media platforms. The side of social media that existed for those magical or supernatural beings, either living in Elsewhere or back in the mortal realms, was more vivid than I had expected. Setting up new profiles and getting connected with people was far easier than I anticipated. Though, I did get a fair number of emails from the various platforms, asking if I were who I said I was. I suppose being considered dead or missing or whatever the mortal realms thought of me set off all sorts of scam alerts.

I had to take new pictures of myself with my phone and scowled at the result. It would have to work for now. I trolled—no pun intended—the platforms for information about Death and made a few notes.

Basically, everyone was terrified of him.

I noticed this because the pictures where Death showed up were at almost ritualistic formal events, and everyone's expression was tense. Or, I think they were tense. It was hard to tell when half of them didn't have humanoid faces. Death didn't appear in the comments or tags at all. Unlike the human side of things, people made no jokes about Death or death or about murder or anything of the sort. They just sort of pretended he didn't exist. I suppose that even among the semi-immortal, Death was the one great equaliser.

I was so engrossed in the new platform WhoWhere —which, surprisingly, did exactly what Yolanda had said—when someone knocked on my door. Loudly. I jerked, flew backwards into my chair and held a hand to my heart. "Don't do that!" I scolded Yolanda.

She looked sheepish, but cleared her throat and stepped aside. "Cal, this is Mercy, from the Order of Silence...she's an, ah, associate of Death."

I stood up as quickly as I could manage and plastered a smile on my face. I hardly noticed the features of the person who glided in. "Welcome! How good of you to come. Please, have a seat."

Mercy moved forwards and I finally noticed her beyond the haze of my excitement. She was exactly what I had expected immortal, magical beings to look like. She was tall and slender, with no small amount of muscle under her medieval-style dress. Her skin was the colour of rich earth and her hair was a shade of white you saw in television. Her face was sharp and solemn, and her eyes shone an iridescent blue. She was beautiful. Inhumanly beautiful. I felt my knees wobbling and the purely male part of my brain sat up to attention.

Mercy moved forwards until she was standing before the chair opposite my desk. She appraised me a moment, eyes piercing. Then, moving more gracefully than most professional dancers, she sat.

"Thank you so much for coming," I said, sitting as well. Yolanda hovered in the background, shifting from foot to foot and looking extremely uncomfortable. I didn't know why. "So, you work with Death?"

"I...contract with him as the occasion calls for it," Mercy said. Her voice was like a whisper of silk over sin and I shivered. "My primary work is with the Order of Silence."

"Er...the Order of Silence?" I asked.

"It is not for you to know, mortal, no matter your role here," Mercy sniffed. I swallowed before I started salivating. Part of me wondered if I should be so eager to talk to this woman, if perhaps there weren't something else going on. That part was really, really quiet.

"Okay," I agreed readily. Perhaps too readily, given my need for information and my lack of understanding about this new world, but there was plenty of time for me to poke around later. "So, what do you do for Death?"

She raised her chin, revealing the smooth lines of her neck. "I am Mercy."

"It's a beautiful name," I agreed. She frowned, the movement not marring her looks at all.

"You do not understand," she scoffed. Yolanda widened her eyes at me and tried to make some sort of gesture with her hands. I stared at her for a moment, understanding something like "bird flies around and dies." I never was very good at charades. I blinked twice, pushed my glasses up my nose and turned back to my conversation with Mercy.

Mercy flicked her eyes to mine and held my stare. The blue seemed to shift colour ever so slightly, the more I looked at it. Each shift was slight, subtle, enough to keep me engrossed. It was mesmerising at first, then a pressure started building behind my eyes. The shades of blue shifted faster, making my head pound as my brain tried to compensate. Nausea built in my stomach. I tried to move away, tried to blink, speak, anything, but I was completely frozen. And I could feel myself needing to beg for release. If I didn't, I would surely endure more pain than I had ever endured before. I would break; nothing would be left of me but a shell.

Mercy blinked and curled her lip, disdainful. The gaze broke and I sucked in a deep breath, my eyes watering.

"I am Mercy," she repeated. "It is not my *name*, human. It is everything I embody."

I managed to swallow down a whimper, but barely. Instead, I sat back in my chair and folded my hands in my lap to keep from trembling. I looked at Yolanda in desperation, hoping that she would have some sort of explanation. The troll woman shuffled forwards, dipping her head respectfully to Mercy as she came within the woman's line of sight.

"She is Death's swiftest," Yolanda said, keeping her eyes fixed firmly on the floor.

"Swiftest what?" I asked. My voice came out in a sort of squeak.

"Assassin," Mercy said. Her voice held the impersonal, emotionless tones you would expect of a stranger passing you in the street. My panting attraction and lust shrivelled up, only to be replaced by a healthy dose of fear.

"I...ah, I see," I said. Mercy raised her eyebrows and blinked slowly. "Death can't do all the work, I suppose."

Mercy coughed out a small laugh. I could see the disdain on her features. "Foolish human, Death does not *kill*."

Maybe it's just the fact that I was human and completely new to this situation, but I was a bit stunned by this revelation. "Uh, what? He's Death! Of course he kills."

"No. Mortals kill. Disease kills. *I* kill. We are tangible. We can affect the world, bring about change," Mercy explained slowly, like I was a child. At this point, I was grateful for any help I could get. "Death is an act. An event. A facilitator."

I nodded. I reached for my keyboard, typing out my notes furiously. Mercy watched with that same disdain. "And that's why he hires you."

"—and me!" a new voice called. A person, just as stunningly beautiful as Mercy, appeared in the doorway. Where Mercy was cold and distant, this man was effusive and almost absurdly cheerful. His colouring was almost the opposite of Mercy's, too, with pale skin and dark brown hair. And, unlike her medieval style of dress, he wore the latest style: slim slacks, a white t-shirt and scarf over that, draped artistically across his shoulders. The odd thing, though, was that where Mercy had eyes that nearly glowed, this man wore a ragged, faded blindfold over his eyes.

"You started without me," he complained, striding in with the same grace as Mercy. He paused beside her chair and gestured to the one in the corner. With a burst of air, it flew over to him and settled down.

There was no hint that he couldn't see because of the blindfold.

Yolanda shifted farther away from the pair of them and muttered something under her breath. "What?" I asked and she blushed. It was an interesting thing to see on a troll. Her cheeks turned a bright shade of green and if she had been remotely human, I would have thought she was going to be ill.

"Don't worry," the newcomer said, flicking his hand dismissively. "Trolls and aurai don't often get along."

"Aurai?" I was beginning to feel like a child thrust into a college astrophysics class.

"Air spirits. Not quite angel-class, but more than mere faeries," the stranger smiled. He leaned forwards and extended his hand. "I'm Justice."

That explained the blindfold.

"Ah, Cal," I said, shaking his hand. His skin was like ice, and tingled with electricity. I tried to discreetly shake my hand under cover of my desk, but I'm fairly certain I failed. "You...you're an assassin too? With the, what is it, Order of Silence?"

Justice threw back his head and laughed. Mercy regarded him with something akin to the look usually reserved for severely decayed bodies. It was the most emotion I had seen from her since our meeting. And no less terrifying. "The *Order*? Please. Those superstitious old bats are so boring. The only good thing about them is dear Mercy here."

"You disrespect the oldest keepers of Rituali in Elsewhere!" Mercy said, her voice heated even if her face didn't show it. Justice made a noise in the back of his throat.

"If you must know, Cal, I don't attach myself to anyone. I work for Death occasionally, but sometimes I work in the legal system. I float around, mostly. Meting out people's just desserts." He flashed his teeth in a predatory smile. I decided that of the two, Mercy was probably my favourite. Justice scared the living daylights out of me.

"Oh, ah, how interesting," I said politely. Marketing, Cal. Public relations. You must keep on these people's good side. If they had one. "So, I asked you here to get a sense of Death. You know he brought me on to be his marketing agent. And to do that, I need to know what he's like. Er, you know."

Both Mercy and Justice gaped at me. Mercy stared with her eyes boring into me and Justice just looked like a fish. "You want to know what *Death* is *like...?*" Mercy said slowly, as if trying to confirm what I was saying. As though the words coming out of my mouth were absolutely insane.

"Marketing campaigns are all about the personal touch," I explained, my smile a touch more forced than it should have been. My cheeks were starting to hurt.

Mercy choked back a sound and Justice just continued to gape. I was just about to launch into my strategy for marketing, starting with my own experiences and what I had gathered so far, when the world—for lack of a better word—shuddered.

I clutched the arms of my chair in desperation.

There was a noise like fingernails on a chalkboard, or bad violin players. I clapped my hands over my ears and promptly fell out of the chair because of it. A moment later, and everything stopped. Silence fell over the room like a heavy blanket.

"What," I panted, clawing my way back into the chair, "was *that*?"

Yolanda swallowed audibly. Justice looked like a wolf, baring his fangs just before eating. Mercy's eyes shone brighter. But both aurai also trembled. Whether in fear, or excitement, I never did find out.

"We'd better get over to the main house," Yolanda said, her voice shaking. Her hands trembled and her eyes were wide, flashing fear.

"Why? What's going on?" I asked. What I really wanted to know was whether I should be running away.

"His wife," Yolanda squeaked.

LIFE AND DEATH

The four of us went to the main house as quickly as possible, not even bothering to lock up after ourselves. Which is to say that Mercy and Justice ran ahead, leaping and running as if they were floating. Yolanda and I took a much slower path, jogging lightly behind them. Or, well, I was jogging lightly. The ground shook beneath Yolanda's feet, almost like it was as scared as she was.

I was so shocked by the idea that Death was *married* that I hardly had time to feel awe over the massive mansion looming in our view. It, like everything else here, was from another time and perfectly preserved. There were carvings and impressive ivy growth and everything that you would expect from an entity as powerful as Death. That wasn't important.

What *was* important was that Yolanda was looking like someone had threatened her. She was obviously terrified. And if someone could scare her, then my own weak, human, killable self should be running away. Fast.

"You're a troll," I said, panting, "shouldn't you be offering to protect me from this?"

Yolanda shot me a wide-eyed look, "Trolls may be scary to humans, but in Elsewhere, we're not the biggest, baddest ones around. I would have thought Justice and Mercy would have clued you in to that."

"Yeah, but they're trained to be super dangerous," I pointed out. We caught up to the two aurai as they were slowing to the front door. Their steps were calm and collected, as if they hadn't run here on the back of the wind. "Surely most people here—"

"You would do well to take heed of the troll's fears, human," Mercy said, smoothing the skirt of her dress. She shifted her shoulders to stand impossibly straighter. Justice just grinned wolfishly again and knocked three times on the massive wooden doors.

I gulped.

Yolanda patted my shoulder, making my already-trembling legs buckle. "Death will protect you."

Yes, because *that* was a comforting thought.

The doors swung open with no one to open them and we stepped inside. The interior of Death's mansion was even more grand than I could have imagined. It was reminiscent of one of the old opera houses or theatres, with marble floors, grand carvings, staircases that spun and twisted magnificently upwards. There were sculptures in many nooks along the wall, some smaller pieces by famous artists. There were paintings on the walls and I was fairly certain that I would never have been able to afford a viewing here, while I was alive and in the mortal realms.

"This way," Justice said, turning down a hallway set behind a hidden door. After we had gotten away from the main room, the house became decidedly more ordinary. Well, if by ordinary you meant an English manor house decked out in the finest fashion. The floors were done in hardwood, there were simple paintings on the wall—all done by masters like Rembrandt and Botticelli—and the furniture was well-used and comfortable. The front of the house was a sham. A facade. And whoever was here—wife of Death or not—was familiar enough with my boss to push right past it.

I definitely felt like I didn't belong.

Blind Justice led us through a maze of corridors until we wound up in a simple living room, of sorts. There were couches and club chairs arrayed near the windows, all done in tasteful leather. The floor boasted a well-worn Persian rug before a massive fireplace. Two of the walls had floor-to-ceiling bookshelves. This was a room for comfort and privacy and never needing to see people you didn't want to see. It was *not* a place for the tension I could feel in the air.

Death was sitting in one of the club chairs, one long leg crossed over the other. He was being confronted by a woman who put Mercy and Justice's beauty to shame. She was tall, full-figured and had an aura of vitality that was impossible to miss. I couldn't tell you what colour her hair was, or whether her skin was light or dark or even a shade of purple. All I knew was that she was stunning and regal. She was the sort of woman you wanted to fight for, to be with, to experience her moods and interests.

I didn't know what Yolanda was on about. This woman wasn't terrifying. She was intoxicating.

Then, she turned around. Her eyes were bright and flashed with more colours than I could name. I felt my heart beating faster. Sweat broke out on my skin. Then, she smiled, showing predatory fangs and hitting me with a wave of pleasure.

"Husband," the woman crooned, glancing over her shoulder at Death, "aren't you going to introduce us?"

Death appraised me and I'm sure he saw how I felt about this woman. But he did no more than sigh and nod slowly. "Very well. My dear, this is Cal Thorpe, my new marketing agent. Cal, this is my wife. Life."

For a second, I couldn't quite process the name. I thought he was just being poetic. Then, I realised, he was being literal. Just like Mercy and Justice, this woman embodied her name. I didn't think she was an aurai or some creature who had adopted the attributes enough to encompass her identity. No, like Death, this woman *was* Life.

"A pleasure," she purred, holding out her hand. I reached for it and, with a blur of motion, found myself being thrown backwards into a chair. Death was on his feet, hands clenched into fists, features twisting into an expression of anger.

"Do not touch him," Death hissed. Life laughed, the sound tinkling and beautiful.

"So possessive," she said. "There's no reason to be. After all, you stole him from me, did you not?"

"Uh, what?" I asked quietly. Yolanda sidled up to me and held a finger to her lips. Got it. Watch, don't interfere. These were heavyweights and I was about as light as a feather by comparison.

"How could I have stolen him from you?" Death asked, regaining his calm. "I took him at the Instant of Death, which is my domain. He was no longer yours."

"But I can feel it," Life said, frowning. "You took his life-force from him. He is immortal, now."

"He works for me," Death replied, sitting back in his chair.

"Oh, please, may I have him?" Life pressed forwards, falling to her knees and draping her hands over Death's knee. The picture of a docile and submissive wife. "Humans are so vital, so *full*. And this one can never die."

"No," Death said in a tone that brooked no nonsense. "He is bound to *me*."

Life snarled and flew backwards, curling her fingers into claws. She drew her shoulders up and I could feel the raw power of hers crackling in the air. Involuntarily, I leaned forwards, wanting to reach out and touch her. To feel her. To be with her. Death frowned, the shadows around him writhing. He raised a hand and dispelled the power, leaving an empty feeling in my chest. No matter that I was bound to Death, I really, really wanted to be with Life.

"Enough of this," Death said. He gestured to a chair and Life huffed, sitting. "Tell me what it is that brought you here. As you can see, I am rather busy."

Life glanced casually over Mercy and Justice and ignored Yolanda completely. "Yes," she snorted, "I can see that. Your hired rabble is here to play."

"And *your* hired rabble," Justice smiled, bowing at the waist. "After all, dear Life, I work for you a good deal of the time."

Life curled her lip and turned her head away. "I suppose. Though you are hardly that helpful. Those pitiful mortals demand justice, demand that I be fair. Foolish, wouldn't you agree?"

Justice flushed and said nothing. Mercy, to her credit, reached out and touched him gently on the arm. Her face still betrayed no emotion. I still found the two of them terrifying, but they suddenly didn't feel like the biggest gun in the room. Whether that was my boss or his wife, though, I didn't know.

All I wanted to do was marketing. Couldn't I just be left alone to do that?

"My dear, please. Your presence is disruptive to my entire realm," Death flicked a piece of dust off his knee, the picture of the long-suffering. "What have you come to say?"

Life huffed, indignant. "Very well," she said. "I want to know why you killed my warrior."

"Your warrior? Another one of your champions?" Death asked.

"Magnus." Life let out a little sigh at the end of his name. "I went to spend the day with him and found that he had died. You *knew* I liked him."

"Magnus? That Norwegian chap? Oh, for goodness sakes, I didn't kill him," Death said. He held up a hand, "Nor did I contract out with anyone to have him killed. Disease made no motions and I would have known if there had been an accident."

Life surged to her feet, seeming to grow taller. Her power crackled around her again, pushing the air out of the room. This time, even Death seemed stunned. Mercy blinked and raised her eyebrows in shock. Justice curled his shoulders forwards. And Yolanda, bless her, stepped slightly in front of me. I just stayed slumped against the couch, deciding that it was probably best I stayed quiet.

"You LIAR!" Life screamed. Her voice split the air and the ground shook again, just as it had in my office. Death clenched his fist and everything stilled, but there was distinct trembling beneath my feet. "Magnus is dead! His belly cut open as he slept! How can you sit there and say you did not kill him?!"

"Because I didn't!" This time Death stood. He faced Life down, his shadows dancing throughout the room. I felt some of the tension disperse and a piece of me relaxed slightly. Death's power, I realised, was making it easier to breathe. To think. I was bound to him, so I felt it.

"Don't think I don't know why you did it," Life stepped forwards, baring her teeth.

"I haven't done it, so stop saying I have," Death growled. He didn't move forwards to counter Life; he just became more solid while everything around him faded slightly. "How can you question this? I am Death. Magnus cannot be dead if I didn't play a part. And I didn't play a part!"

"I know you are lying," Life snapped. "But of course you would deny it, *Husband*. Don't you hate me enough? Do you have to ruin everything I have, too?"

"I am perfectly happy with our arrangement. You stay away from me and I stay away from you. We only have to meet at official functions. If you thought I hated you that much, then why would I do something that would bring you here?" Death stood taller, but he still looked up to the engorged figure of Life. She snarled a wordless sound and spun around, pacing the room.

"Because I loved Magnus," she said, turning violently as she stalked towards the other end of the room. "And you couldn't possibly stand to see me happy."

"That is ridiculous," Death scoffed. "Why do I care if you loved him? The mortal would have come to me in the end. They all do."

Life screamed again, lunging for Death, nails poised for clawing. Death just extended one hand and Life stopped in her tracks, completely immobilised. His mouth tightened into a thin line and the empty holes that were his eyes darkened with shadow. "Do not presume to test me," he said, his voice low and furious. "I have listened to you ranting about your lost warrior, but no more. I tell you I did not do it."

"Bastard," Life hissed as he released her. She clenched her fists and looked like she was about to burst into flames. Then, her nostrils flared and she turned to me. A cruel, ruthless smile curled up her features. "Fine. If you can prove that you didn't kill Magnus, then I'll accept your word. If not, then I will do everything in my power to destabilise your realm."

"And how would you suggest I prove this?" Death said softly, incredulously.

Life jerked her head in my direction, "You hired a marketing agent to protect your image. Use him."

Then, she did burst into flames. Actual flames, bright enough that even after I closed my eyes the afterimage burned. When I could open my eyes again and see, the living room was still in one piece. There was a scorch mark in the rug, but it was being slowly repaired by tiny wisps of shadow.

Death sighed and sat back in his chair. He said nothing for a moment, then, "I really didn't have anything to do with the death of her warrior."

Mercy said nothing. Justice opened his mouth, then changed his mind and shrugged. "How could you not have? You're Death. Anything that dies or crosses over or whatever is part of your domain," Justice said.

"It is not an easy task," Death said, "but it is possible. It has been done."

"Really?" I asked. Everyone turned and looked at me. Okay, not a great time for asking questions. "Sorry," I muttered.

"No, you have a right to know," Death said. "You will be the one responsible for solving this...murder."

I blinked. I looked up at Yolanda, who also blinked. I blinked again. "You can't be serious," I said.

"Perfectly serious," Death replied. "My other employees have a, hmmm, vested interest in my line of work. You are the only one who does not. And, being human, you have a free license to go anywhere and ask questions. No one will think anything of it, given how unusual a human in Elsewhere is."

"Like an idiotic foreigner who can't find his way to the bus stop," I said. Death smiled, though the smile didn't quite reach his empty eyes.

"Precisely," he said.

"You do realise I'm not an investigator. I've never had training, never worked on anything remotely close to an investigation. I do marketing and publicity, which is completely different. I don't even like cop shows!" I said.

"Yolanda will render her assistance," Death said.

"I haven't had training either," Yolanda said, though the words were hardly more than a whisper.

Death sighed and leaned back in his club chair. "I would not ask this of you unless I were desperate. My wife cannot actually kill *me* or do me direct harm, but she can make it very difficult for my subjects and my realm. And if she starts challenging me on every circumstance of a mortal dying, then I will have to take drastic action."

"Drastic action?" I asked before I could clamp my mouth shut over the question. I really didn't want to know, but sometimes my curiosity is a lot faster than my brain.

Death looked into the fireplace. The flames took on a black tinge and the temperature plummeted. "The last instance resulted in World War II."

"Ah," I said weakly. I looked up at Yolanda. She looked stunned. In fact, she looked so stunned that she stomped over to the other end of the couch and sat down. My end of the couch rose off the ground about a foot or so and I slid into her.

"I think this is going to be a lot of trouble," she said frankly.

"I think you're probably right," Death agreed. The both of them looked at me.

I replied with a half-smile. "I guess your social media pages can wait."

DEAD MAN WALKING

"**I** have no idea what I'm doing," I said nearly an hour later. Yolanda was sitting across from me in my office, holding a notebook on her lap. Mercy and Justice had vanished after our little debacle, going back to wherever it was they went to warn whoever they knew about the conflict between Life and Death. Or so I imagined by the frightened looks they were wearing as they vanished in a burst of wind. Death had ignored Yolanda and I after our unfortunate conscription, instead brooding before the fireplace. I didn't yet know him well enough to determine if that was normal. He seemed the sort, but after being challenged like that by an equally terrifying and dangerous being, I figured I would be brooding, too.

I would have much preferred cowering in my bed under the covers until the encounter became a distant memory, but instead I was in my office, trying to figure out how to solve a murder when it couldn't have been Death.

"I mean, where do you even *start* to investigate a murder?"

Yolanda tapped her mouth with the end of a pen. The writing instrument was dwarfed by her enormous hand and yet her handwriting still managed to be neater and smaller than mine. Some things just aren't fair. "Well, the people in the television shows usually start with information about the victim."

I latched onto her words like a lifeline. "Yes! Yes, we'll do that. How do we do that? I mean, are we assuming that someone supernatural had something to do with this or that it was someone in my world. I mean, the mortal realm? Wait, he *was* human, right?"

"Yes. Life's champions are usually human. And if Death didn't know about it, then someone from Else-where had to be involved," Yolanda pointed out. I felt like an idiot. Of course some big baddy had to be involved. My life was never going to be simple again.

I leaned back in my chair. "You want me to put together a marketing campaign, no problem. Create advertisements that have a great click rate? Give me an hour. Deal with smear tactics against my clients? Sure, easy. But this? I am way, way out of my depth. I hardly even know what's going on except Life and Death are at each other's throats and you and I are caught in the middle. Oh, and there are aurai and trolls and the possibility of the next world war is at my feet. My goodness, it's like a completely foreign language, in the middle of a firefight!"

Yolanda shifted in her chair and said nothing. I sighed.

"Alright, fine. I suppose we'll have to go make a visit to Life and ask her about Magnus," I said. Yolanda licked her lips nervously.

"We could...go talk to..." Yolanda struggled to come up with another person we could interview. We didn't even have enough to know Magnus' last name, only that he was Norwegian and had been eviscerated.

"Face it," I said, feeling a ball of nervousness in my stomach, "we're going to have to talk to Life. She was the one who cared."

"I don't like leaving Death's realms. Except to visit Graveltoes. But there's bad things out there," Yolanda whispered. I, oddly enough, was very interested to see what was beyond my boss' lands. The thought of having to explore made this whole murder situation far more bearable. So far upon arrival, I had been poked by unidentified creatures, talked to assassins who probably wouldn't hesitate to kill me, and been handed a job I couldn't understand, nor did I really want. The alternative, though, was much worse. And this was only my second day here. I wanted to see those things I had glimpsed outside the car's windows on my trip here. I wanted to learn more about Elsewhere. The sooner I got this investigation over with, the sooner I could get on with my new life.

But Yolanda was obviously scared. So, like the

sympathetic boss I am, I nodded in understanding and made her help me anyways. "I'm afraid we'll have to leave Death's lands, though. The answers are out there, not in here. How do we get around? Is there a way to contact Ygg...Egg....the chauffeur?'

"Yggdral works for Death," Yolanda rubbed her foot over the floor, not meeting my eyes. "He won't go anywhere unless its official. This is very...not official."

"And what does that mean?" I asked slowly. Yolanda frowned and looked studiously at the floor.

"We'll have to take...we'll have to go by wyvern," she said.

"Uh... what?"

"Wyvern. They're trained to carry up to seven people," Yolanda grumbled. "They're the most reliable way of transportation if you don't have a car and you don't have magic."

I knew she was unhappy. Everything I had seen thus far indicated that I should listen to Yolanda, that her instincts and fears were accurate, but I couldn't help myself. I pushed my glasses up my nose and grinned.

—

IT BECAME apparent almost as soon as we got to the wyvern station why Yolanda hated it. The wyvern was large, scaly, and with many pointy bits. It had massive claws on its back feet and its wings were tipped in claws that were even larger, like they were compensating for only having one set of legs. Their tails, too, were tipped in spikes that looked like they would impale you faster than blinking. A set of wooden stairs was wheeled over to the side of the wyvern. It flushed a deep red then settled back into the sort of greyish blue that I had first seen. I looked up at the massive box strapped to the creature's back and discovered a few problems. First, the seats were made for people of relatively normal size. Yolanda was quite a bit bigger than that. But, more than that, we would be sitting in the open air, barely strapped in. The wyvern wasn't like a bus, either. It *moved*. It was extremely disconcerting to be jostled up and down or side to side every time the wyvern shifted.

They were fascinating creatures, though. I climbed up the steps and sat in the seat next to Yolanda, peering over the side of the box at the ground some many feet below. "Are all dragons this big?" I asked. I must have said it too loudly, because nearly everyone froze and turned their heads to look at me.

"Cal," Yolanda said quietly, tying the leather straps as tightly as they would go. "Wyverns and dragons are *not* the same thing. Wyverns have two legs and are a lot more, ah, bestial in nature. Dragons are magically gifted and would slaughter you alive—slowly—for comparing them to wyverns."

"Why? They're just animals," I said. I shrugged, "Okay, they're really cool, magical animals, but still."

Yolanda bared her teeth in what was closest to a grimace. "Don't tell any dragon that. Ever."

"Indeed," a voice said. A person sitting in front of us turned and looked at me with thinly disguised contempt. He was pasty white with dark hair and eyes shadowed by an overly large fedora. He wore a white suit, which somehow managed to clash with his skin, and gloves on his hands. In fact, every part of him except his face was covered by something, and that was set in shadow. And, if that weren't obvious enough, when he smiled at my ignorance, there were fangs showing. I didn't bother asking Yolanda any questions, deciding it might be better to keep my ignorance about, well, everything to myself. I figured I'd wait and see what happened. We wouldn't want me reduced to a pile of dust because I'd mistaken a goblin or something for a vampire.

"Dragons are some of the most intelligent beings known in Elsewhere," the man continued in a smooth drawl. It was probably meant to be superior or intimidating or something, but I did not much notice. "They only resemble wyverns in looks. They're certainly not related."

"Thanks for the tip," I said, doing my best to maintain my polite smile. These people had nothing on Old Lady Harcourt, I thought. She would have this vampire in a puddle of apology within thirty seconds.

"You must be new to be so stupid," the man said. "Or were you brought along for the troll's snack?"

"Actually, I'm the new marketing and publicity

agent for Death," I said cheerfully. I held out my hand. "Cal Thorpe. And this is my assistant, Yolanda."

For some strange reason, this introduction caught the man's attention. He perked up and took my hand eagerly. "A pleasure, Cal. May I call you Cal? Oh, wonderful! I'm Prince Thaddeus Bartholomew Yannick Wentworth, of the House Vampyr. You're a marketing agent, you say?"

"I am," I nodded. "I deal with pretty much anything my clients need. Public relations, image boosting, social media marketing and branding, general marketing campaigns. I can find the best way to make a person look fantastic at events. I've done poster design and advertisements and...well, I mean that's what I *used* to do. It's a bit different, here. I'm not doing much marketing at the moment. I'm still settling in..."

I didn't want to get too involved in my current problems. Who knew what the people in Elsewhere would say when they learned of what had happened? I didn't even know if this sort of thing was normal. Did people know about the broken marriage of Life and Death? Did people care about supernatural occurrences that were far from what I imagined were usual? I realised, just then, how much research I had to do. It was like starting my entire understanding of the world from scratch.

"That's such a shame," Prince Thaddeus said. "If you ever want to get back into marketing, then *please* let me know."

"Er, okay?" I said, slightly confused. Yolanda said

nothing, which was either a sign that I should stop talking or a sign that I was doing something completely harmless.

"It's so difficult to get a good idea of who we are when you can't even take a picture of us! No social media updates, except boring text. And who wants to read that when they could look at a picture? And not to mention that we can't even look in mirrors to figure out if what we're wearing looks good on us. We have to rely on everyone else to tell us," Thaddeus complained, waving his hands dramatically.

I exchanged a look with Yolanda, who shrugged.

"There was this one time that my aunt Margery had to be at a Faerie Solstice ball and ended up the butt of everyone's jokes. Her brother—not my father—had decided to tell her that she looked wonderful in a bright yellow monstrosity. It was horrible."

"I imagine," I said. I must have looked quite puzzled, because Prince Thaddeus threw back his head and started laughing. I noticed that when he did, not even a little bit of his skin touched the sunlight. That was quite the hat.

"You must be confused," he said, purring like a cat. "But the fact is, most of the mortal stories have it wrong. Yes, we're put off by garlic and wooden stakes and crosses and all that, but we're also incredibly vain. It's a by-product of not being able to see what you look like in a world of beautiful things. We want to be beautiful as well. So people like you—who deal with image and perception—are like jewels to us."

"That is both gratifying and terrifying," I said with my best cheerful smile. Yolanda nudged me with her elbow. I winced and glared at her. She widened her eyes, probably as a warning.

"Oh, don't worry," Thaddeus said. "We don't kill people like you. You're too valuable."

I was about to say something more, expressing relief, when Yolanda cut in, her voice sharp, "But you can enthral them."

I recoiled and looked up at my assistant in shock. "Enthral?"

"They used to require a taste of your blood," Yolanda spat, "but now it is easy enough to mesmerise with the voice. A whisper here, a word in the ear there and your free will goes away."

Thaddeus looked like he was about to say something when the wyvern lurched. I surged back against the seat, my head jerking. No sooner than I had gotten a breath in and the wyvern lurched again. Two flaps of the enormous wings out to either side and we were airborne. The wind, thankfully, became too loud for any real conversation, not to mention I had to focus on catching my breath.

Yolanda did lean over and shout something in my ear, "Try not to get eaten! Death would be very unhappy."

Ah, yes, well.

After about thirty seconds, I discovered another reason why Yolanda hated wyvern-travel. It was appalling. Unlike an airplane, the ride was not smooth at all. You jerked up whenever the creature flapped and back down on the upstroke. The leather straps across my hips felt frighteningly insecure in holding me in place. I couldn't hear anything and I'm fairly certain that if I opened my mouth, a bug would fly in at the wrong moment. If there were even bugs in the Elsewhere.

That was a cheering thought, which made me smile for much of the remainder of the trip.

Yolanda sat next to me with her hand pressed firmly over her mouth and looking far more green than she normally did. I really hoped she wasn't going to be sick.

Finally, we landed. I lurched from the seat as quickly as I could, staggered down the wooden steps, and fell to the ground with all the grace of a dying cat. Yolanda, at least, wasn't any more graceful. Thaddeus and the other passengers, however, descended with immortal elegance. The vampire prince helped me to my feet.

"I promise not to enthral you," he said, holding up his hands in innocence. "You work for far to powerful a being to risk it. Just…"

"Just what?" I gurgled, feeling my own stomach settle back into place.

"If you don't mind taking on a few more clients…or if you have any tips?"

I will say this: the poor vampire looked desperate. And given the fact that his suit clashed with his very skin and his hair sported an unusual shape, even under the hat, I couldn't blame him. I sighed and looked around, making sure Yolanda wasn't going to sneak up on me. She was still a ways off, resting her head against a tree. "Alright. Fine. I will say this: have you considered hiring an artist?"

"An artist?" Thaddeus looked shocked.

"Sure. Digital technology lets some artists paint photo-realistic images. You get enough of them and you could create a whole slew of portraits. It wouldn't be as fast as a picture, but even a five-minute sketch would be something."

Thaddeus widened his eyes and grinned, showing off those fangs again. I took a step back. He shook my hand vigorously and marched away, looking like I had handed him a gold medal. A moment later and he winked out of existence. I cleaned the lenses of my glasses and looked again, but my eyes had not deceived me. The vampire was gone.

Yolanda reached me at last, scowling in distaste at the wyvern. "Welcome to the Land of the Living," she grumbled, waving an arm.

I looked around and whistled in appreciation. It was almost the mirror image of Death's lands, but where everything there was grey and silver and white and black, here there was colour everywhere. The leaves on the trees sported a more vibrant array of greens than anything I had ever seen. The sky was intensely blue and everywhere I looked, life thrived. Birds sang. Deer grazed on the grass next to the resting wyvern, completely unconcerned by its presence. I was fairly certain I saw people dressed in green and brown flitting through the trees.

"Wow," I said. "It's—"

"Saturated," Yolanda said in distaste. "Come on," she said. "Let's go find the palace."

I put my hands in my pockets, kicked my feet over the blades of grass and happily followed my angry assistant to go find the Halls of Life.

The house was even more grand than Death's manor, which would have seemed impossible had I not witnessed it firsthand. There were turrets and enormous stained glass windows and, except for the fact that it was too modern, I would have called it a castle. Or, as Yolanda had said, a palace.

Inside, there were too many people hanging about in various stages of partying for me to notice much of the decor. I saw small people with bird wings laughing together by a fountain pouring out champagne. Yolanda sniffed and said, "Cherubs. All drunk."

There were vampires dancing together in a candle-lit room. I only knew them as vampires because they were dressed extravagantly and had absolutely no sense of fashion. That, and I thought I caught a glimpse of Prince Thaddeus whispering excitedly with a short, squat woman. Then there were beings of extreme grace in various colours—pale white, green, brown, blue— and an aura of power about them that I studiously avoided. There were elves with their pointed ears and cat-slanted eyes. I even saw a being that looked very similar to Graveltoes, if he had been twice as tall.

Everyone was either laughing or drinking or dancing. There were musicians playing and games going on. The music style changed as you went from room to room, leaping through jazz to disco to country. My ears started pounding by the time we made it through the front half of the palatial house. I was handed a drink by a laughing woman with curling goat's horns, the smile on her face too broad to be natural. I saw people sleeping happily on couches and others carrying plates of food. The entire house was one long, never-ending party, I discovered. People coming and going as they chose. It was full of life.

And it was too loud.

Yolanda and I managed to snag a haggard looking footman to take us to Life, and were directed to a long gallery at the back of the house, well away from the rooms of partying people. As soon as the doors closed behind us the sounds from the rest of the house faded away completely. The long hallway was framed by tall windows on one side and portraits on the other. A strip of plush, bright red carpet, muffled what little sound did slip into the hall. The gallery was lit only by whatever sun streamed through the windows, though that was enough to feel bright and energetic. The light fell upon the portraits, done in a number of styles. I looked at one of them and blinked in surprise.

It was of a human.

She was beautiful, in a perfectly ordinary sort of way. Her hair was bright, vibrant red and she wore clothing that was probably early Native American.

Next to her picture was one of a man wearing the clothes I would attribute to early Scottish. And another, next to his. All the way down the gallery, enormous pictures covered the walls, all of humans.

Frankly, it was a little creepy.

Yolanda and I found Life standing before the last portrait in the gallery, next to a door gilded with gold leaf. She stood there with a quiet fury radiating out, her arms wrapped around her and her very breath making the air crackle.

"So he sent you, then," Life hissed, not turning her attention away from the picture for a moment. I risked stepping a few inches forwards to get a good look. The picture was of a man in modern dress: jeans and a fisherman's sweater. He had blonde hair, green eyes and the look of someone who could get into trouble just by smiling. A trickster, if ever there was one.

"Is this…?" I asked.

"Magnus," Life said, her voice sharpening over the second syllable. "My beloved champion."

"Champion?" I frowned. He looked more like a boater to me. Maybe he had some sort of hidden martial arts talent.

Life curled her lip and deigned to glance in my direction. I immediately wished she hadn't. Her gaze flattened me, literally. I fell to the ground and struggled to breathe, to move. Yolanda let out a strangled sound and I could see her also struggling against some invisible force out of the corner of my eye. After half a minute or so, Life clicked her tongue and shook her head. The pressure lessened enough to allow me a gasping breath.

I coughed and spluttered my way into standing and moved quickly to go stand by Yolanda. It seemed safer to be far away from Life.

"You wouldn't know what it is to be my warrior, my champion," Life sneered. "Not when you gave up so easily on your own life. Don't you know most people survive a single bullet wound? And it was on your right side. You would have been rushed to the hospital. Who knows, you might have lived. But you chose instead to give up."

"Uh, what? How do you know about—"

"Just as my husband," Life spat the word, "knows when people die, or are near to dying, so do I know when people give up on me. On life. My warriors, though, fight for it with every last breath in their body. They want to experience the world. They want to live with their entire soul. They are my favoured ones."

"So you give them an unfair advantage?" That just seemed like cheating to me. "Give them what they want?"

Life tilted back her head and let out a single bark of laughter. "You are ignorant if you think that it is in my nature to do such a thing. Don't you know Life isn't fair? That when something bad happens, people have to pick themselves up and say 'that's Life?' Life is a cruel mistress. But Life is worth pursuing. And my warriors, no matter how cruel or unfair or wrong I may be, woo me anyways. And I love them for it."

That was a little disturbing. "You only favour those who *fight* you? That seems a bit...conflict-oriented," I said. Life flashed her teeth in a smile I now realised was cunning and cruel. The hair on the back of my neck stood straight up.

"You finally understand, human," she said, turning away from the picture to prowl towards me. Yolanda let out a quiet whimper and drew back a few steps. I didn't blame her. Life stopped mere inches from me, invading every bit of personal space I had and setting off alarm bells in my head. I was pretty certain that if I fled, though, this whole discussing Magnus thing could be thrown out. Part of me didn't care. I would happily have given up on this investigation to go back to Death's lands and let some other fool figure this out. Except the world would burn if I did.

Life drew a hand down my arm, the touch feather light. My hands started to shake.

"If I am not conflict, then what am I?" Life whispered in my ear.

"Terrifying," I said, before I could stop myself. Life laughed and stepped back enough to let me breathe.

"You *are* amusing. I see why Death picked you." Life turned back to her portrait. It was a pretty clear dismissal. Only, I hadn't gotten what I came for and I really, really hated that.

"Actually, we came to ask you about Magnus," I said. An instant later and the air was sucked from the room. The light outside the windows darkened and Yolanda squeaked in terror. Or maybe that was me.

"You dare," Life snarled, tendrils of light swirling about her just as Death's shadows did. "You, an emissary of the one who took Magnus from me!"

"But that's the point," I said, barely managing to speak the words. "Death didn't do it. And he wants me to prove it. So I thought the best way to do that would be to get to know the victim."

Life hissed through her teeth. She drew herself up, fairly towering over me. "You wish to know Magnus? Very well, then."

Life moved towards me, hand stretched out. Yolanda let out a cry of alarm and I could hear her thudding steps as she moved towards me. I was entranced, though, and couldn't move. Life just got closer and closer, until her index finger was a breath away from my forehead. With an angry laugh, Life touched me and the world fell away.

LIFE AFTER DEATH

*T*he first thing I noticed was pain. It radiated through my veins, burning into my bones and making every nerve ending feel as though it had been doused in fire. This was like what had happened when Death shook my hand, except I didn't think that I was being separated from my life-force. No, this time, I was fairly certain that Life was encouraging the pain. Any prolonged contact with her and I would probably go mad.

The pain lessened and I took in great gulps of breath. I was standing on a hill, the grass short and interspersed with rocks. It wasn't quite right, though. Wherever I looked, things were just a touch translucent. I reached out a hand and touched the ground and, sure enough, it passed right through the blades of grass.

"It is a memory, idiot human." Life's voice rang harsh in my ear, echoing inside my head. I straightened, pushing up my glasses, and saw her standing on the hill next to me. She was looking down the slope to where a form was sitting, hunched over an object in his lap. I recognised the man from the portrait. This was Magnus.

He was wearing all black and had a black balaclava sitting on the ground beside him. Life walked towards him and I followed. We circled around Magnus until we could see what he was doing. I was struck again by his mischievous looks. Like a child who snuck cookies from the jar and didn't get caught. Or a person whose business laundered money for the mob. Or, as it turned out, a jewel thief.

Magnus was sitting on an outcropping of rock and had spread an array of jewellery out before him. There were three necklaces with diamonds and emeralds and sapphires and rubies, a collection of bracelets, some rings and earrings and two watches. Magnus was grinning widely, stroking a light hand over each of the pieces.

"You and I, we're going to go places," he said. Well, sort of. What he actually said was in a different language. Norwegian, I guessed, since that was how Death had described him. But the words that my brain actually processed were English. It was like a little translator lived in my ear, whispering the words. Actually, it was sort of like watching a news interview with someone speaking a different language.

I rubbed at my ear, trying to make the itch go away. Life snorted and shook her head at me. She folded her arms and focused her attention on Magnus, her eyes a little sad and a lot angry.

"We're going to find a nice place for you to go and I'm going to live like a king. Those idiots in the police don't know anything. They think it was an inside job. Ha! As if any of those buffoons could come up with something this clever." Magnus laughed, the sound echoing off the hills around him. We were in the middle of nowhere and there probably wasn't a person around for miles. Not to mention a road. No wonder he hadn't been caught.

"He was the most clever thief," Life sighed. "Pitting his intelligence against some of the great detectives and technology of this age. And never once did they even suspect him. He fought tooth and nail for what he wanted, doing everything in his power to be better than everyone else. Smarter. Faster. More nimble. More capable. He was one of the best of my champions."

I think I understood, though it made my stomach roil. Life was like those Roman emperors who thrilled to see the gladiators fighting it out in the ring. They cheered as the blood spilled and lives were lost. And those who made it to the top were rewarded.

I decided to speak up before Life snapped out of her little swoon over Magnus and started yelling at me again. "Uh, I hate to, you know, but...how did he die?"

There was another burst of pain and we were suddenly somewhere else. Life threw her arm out and gestured, face twisted into a bestial snarl. "Like *this*," she said.

We were standing in a cabin. At least, it looked like a cabin. The walls were made of wood and stone and the roof was too low for modern comfort. There was a fireplace in one corner, the flames still flickering. A bed was close to the fireplace with a table and small stove on the opposite side of the room. There was a door and two windows, and that was it. A simple life reminiscent of a time far in the past, meant for getting away from the world. Perfect for camping or hunting. Or running from the police.

Magnus' body was sprawled across the threshold of the door. He was lying on his back, his eyes staring in horror at something long gone. His mouth hung slack jawed and his blonde hair was splattered with red. There was no more mischief in his expression. Only pain and fear.

I looked a little farther down the body and felt my stomach recoil. Magnus had been eviscerated. Literally. It was one thing to have been told this, but another to see it in person. I swallowed down bile. His intestines and stomach and other organs were strewn across him, the blood dried and turning brown. His legs were sticking out at awkward angles, as if he had tried to turn and run and found nowhere to go. Flies were gathering on his body in a dark cloud.

I turned back into the cabin and tried not to retch. This was just a memory, I told myself. There nothing here that could harm me. I mean, I couldn't even smell the body. I tried to tell myself it was just a movie. A really bad movie. But no movie I had ever seen had a body that looked quite so real.

"I found him like this," Life said, her voice dry, her face twisted with disappointment. "If I had come earlier, I might have seen who killed him. But I can only show you what I found."

"I'm sorry," I managed, looking anywhere but at the body. "Really, I am."

"And yet you still persist in this fallacy that my husband was not involved," Life scoffed. She waved a hand and the world fell into pain once again. When I came to myself, I was leaning against the wall, gasping for breath. Yolanda was keeping me from falling to the floor completely, a scowl on her features.

"You should not have touched him," she said to Life.

"I merely showed him the truth." Life lifted a single shoulder in a shrug and turned back to her portrait. I saw her mouth tighten at the corners and knew she was trying to rid herself of the image of Magnus' body. I doubted she would be able to do so.

"It's alright, Yolanda," I wheezed. I pushed myself off the wall and straightened, one arm supported by my assistant. "I think I got all the information I could."

"Do not return unless you wish to denounce my husband," Life said, voice cold. I ducked my head in some sort of respectful nod and turned away. Yolanda helped me totter back down the long gallery and we never once looked back.

The troll woman spoke after we closed the door

behind us and the noises of the house had returned in full force. "What did you learn?" Yolanda asked in a low voice.

"I think this is going to be a lot more complicated than I thought," I said just as softly. I waited until we were well away from that gallery before I told Yolanda what had happened. She tugged on an ear nervously and looked around.

We were alone—or as alone as you could get in a house as busy as Life's. We were in a room floored with marble, with high ceilings and furniture strewn about in random formation. There was a female satyr draped over a couch, giggling incoherently at another satyr's words. Three diminutive faeries were dancing around in circles, shrieking in delight. Music came from a corner where some hunched figure was leaning over an honest-to-goodness jukebox.

Yolanda and I sat on one of the couches and put our heads together so we wouldn't be overheard. Though I doubted that anyone in the room would want to bother with us when they were too busy drinking in Life's essence. Death had no place here, so we were invisible.

Yolanda shook her head. "I don't like it."

"Well, there's not a whole lot I can do about that. I didn't get any clues as to who killed Magnus. He was a jewel thief, and apparently a good one, but evisceration seems a little extreme."

"It is a common happening, when the immortals get angry at mortals. You are so fragile," Yolanda said. Gee, way to make me feel better. "No, she *touched* you. That is very, very bad."

"What? Oh, you mean Life. Why is that so bad? I mean, it hurt. A lot. But I'm not dead. And there are no lasting effects, right?" I tried to smile encouragingly, but Yolanda was worrying me. "Right?!"

"Life and Death hold more power than any other being I have ever known," Yolanda whispered. "Even the immortals must fall to their power. There are very few who don't have to worry about truly dying, and therefore need not bother with Life interfering in their existence. Her touch...it amplifies her power a thousand-fold. She's like a...what do you call it? Those big explody things that make the plant-clouds?"

"A nuclear bomb? A mushroom cloud?"

Yolanda nodded. "Her touch devastates, because people cannot handle so much concentrated life. It's like...everything happens all at once and your brain overloads and then your body overloads and then everything goes explody."

"So I should be a burnt-up crisp on the ground, is what you're saying," I said flatly. Yolanda plucked at her shirt and grimaced. But she nodded. "Oh, good. Seeing as I'm not a burnt up crisp on the ground and I feel pretty normal—circumstances notwithstanding—I'll worry about that later. Right now, we need to figure out who killed Magnus. Then we can get as far away from here as soon as possible and I can go on with my marketing."

"But, Cal—"

"No." I held up a hand. "You are my assistant and must do what I say. I say we're going to figure this out. Got it?"

Yolanda huffed. "Fine."

"Good. So. If we can't figure out who killed Magnus based on his apparently-common-when-immortals-get-involved wounds, then we'll have to go about this another way," I said. I mulled the thoughts over in my mind and watched the satyrs pour wine down their throats, dizzyingly drunk and stupidly alive. "Who would want to hurt Life badly enough to kill her warrior? Or, was it Death they were after?"

Yolanda may have looked like a creature who wouldn't be able to do much math, but she was incredibly quick. "We figure out who wanted to hurt Life, or Death, and then we'll figure out why Magnus was killed."

"Exactly. Who do you know that has a grudge against Life? Or Death," I added as an afterthought. This seemed more like a direct attack at Life to me, but I supposed I couldn't rule the other side out. I was way, way behind any understanding of any Elsewhere politics.

"If someone is subverting Death's power, then the balance is affected," Yolanda said. I gave her my best confused expression. She cleared her throat and took another look around the room. The hunched figure by the jukebox swayed in time to the music—a jazz rendition of the BeeGees—and the faeries had spun themselves into a stupor. We were being ignored completely.

"The balance," Yolanda explained, "between Life and Death is crucial. Without Death, Life would go on everlasting."

"Isn't that what the immortals are doing?" I asked.

Yolanda shook her head. "The immortals can die. They don't die of old age or minor disease, but they can die. They can be actively killed. They can be brought down by a plague on their magic. They can fade into nothingness when their existence is forgotten by even themselves. It seldom happens, but it is possible."

"Okay. So everlasting Life means that everyone just keeps going. No chance of Death. Wouldn't loads of people want that?" I asked. I mean, really. Human doctors had been trying to figure out how to keep from dying for ages. Look at the rise in plastic surgery, if you had any doubts. Look at what I did to keep on living, for that matter.

Yolanda's mouth tightened at the edges. "It would be...bad. The conflict that Life provides would rise to exponential scales. There would be war without end. No matter how many times you killed a soldier, she would keep rising from the ground. Elsewhere and the mortal realms would become nothing but endless carnage and temptation and revelry."

"People would go mad," I said softly.

"So there is balance. Necessary balance. But, if Death becomes the stronger, then society would be culled. Populations would plummet and entire species would cease to exist," Yolanda said.

"The world could start over," I breathed. Yolanda nodded and looked at her hands. I had this impression that she was always too nervous. That things surely couldn't be that bad. She jumped at every unusual noise, freaked out during my interactions with Mercy and Justice, was terrified of Life. But whenever she explained things, her nervousness made perfect sense.

I hated it.

"Okay, fine." I leaned my elbows on my knees and stared at the room. It was as though I didn't even exist. The moment the creatures moved in my direction, some invisible force turned them away. I imagined that this was something to do with my being bound to Death. Life's presence in his realm had caused an upset. Could my presence in Life's realm be doing something subtler?

I took a breath. "Who would *want* to cause an apocalypse? Who would benefit if everyone started dying off?"

Yolanda shrugged. "I don't know. I'm only an assistant. I don't have any experience in this sort of thing."

"You've given a whole lot of theory so far," I pointed out.

"That's just general knowledge. *Everyone* knows that," Yolanda said.

"Okay, then we'll have to talk to someone who knows more than general knowledge," I said. Yolanda's eyes widened and her greyish skin paled to a frightening degree. She shook her head violently. "Surely you know of someone who could help."

"No," Yolanda said firmly. She tightened her hands into fists on the couch cushion and I saw fabric start to tear. I winced, but we had to do this. The alternative was, as I feared, really, really bad. Because my not-quite-afterlife couldn't be *normal*.

"So you're just going to let this happen. Start an apocalypse," I said. "The end of everything."

She bit her lip, showing off her teeth. I watched her, not looking away and giving her a chance to consider another option. I had to have this information. Yolanda would just have to get over it.

"There is...a sage. Of sorts," Yolanda started. She furrowed her brow and looked at me desperately. I said nothing. "He lives at the top of a mountain near Death's realm. It is not hard to find."

"So why are you so scared, then?" I straightened in the chair, fixing Yolanda with my best stern-boss stare. She shuddered, the movement going straight from her head to her toes.

"Because of the cost," she murmured. "He will ask a price. And you must be willing to pay it."

"And if I'm not?" I said carefully.

"Then he will kill you for wasting his time," Yolanda said, her words barely a breath in the air.

Ah. Well.

Why couldn't these people just want like a pretty please, a free sandwich, and maybe some favour for the future? Why did everything have to be bloody and violent and too much drinking and life or assassins from The Order of Silence? I guess when you're relatively immortal, some things become more important than others. And sandwiches didn't make that list.

"Then I'd better be willing to pay the price," I said. Yolanda let out a small cry and the satyrs looked distastefully in our direction, the first time they had actively noticed us. Yolanda and I waited, not breathing, until they looked away, though I don't know why we were so nervous about anyone overhearing. No one else would be stupid enough to get involved in stopping the apocalypse.

"Look, I know that you're scared. But we need this information. Or, besides the end of the world, we'd be letting Death down. He hired me to help protect his image and that's exactly what I'm going to do. You don't have to come, if you don't want."

"I'd rather not," Yolanda said. She clapped a hand over her mouth and looked at me, pained. "I'm sorry."

"No, it's alright," I put a hand on her knee in comfort, though I'm not sure it worked. "You just tell me where to go and what to do and I'll take care of it."

"It's just...my cousin went to ask him a question once," Yolanda said, looking at her hands in her lap. "The price he asked was the use of my cousin's right hand. Three days later, his right hand strangled his wife."

I was pretty sure my mouth fell open. "Okay then. I understand why you don't want to go."

"But you're going to do it anyways." It wasn't a question and I didn't give an answer. Just shrugged. Yolanda nodded and we left the drunk satyrs and dancing faeries in peace.

It wasn't hard to get on the wyvern again, knowing that what was coming was far worse than flying. True, it was still pretty horrible. But the ride felt like it was over too quickly. We were maybe a few hundred metres from Death's realm when the wyvern landed. I could see the silvery trees and a part of me wanted to go and shelter under them. I could tell Death what I had learned and he could make the bargain with whatever sage this was. I could go focus on my marketing.

And fail in the first real task I had been set. I would ruin Death's chance at maintaining his image before I even started. I didn't think I was really that cowardly. And I was probably more curious about this sage than was healthy.

Call it a condition, curiosity.

Yolanda hiked with me to the base of the mountain. It wasn't an enormous mountain, more like a slag of rock that had been driven from the ground during a volcanic eruption. There were enough plants in a mixture of the over-saturated variety from Life's lands with the silvery-grey types from Death's lands. Everything was perfectly still, like the world was holding its breath and waiting for some idiot—that would be me— to climb to their doom. My troll assistant, tall and massive and terrified, pointed to the path that would take me up and took two definitive steps back. I started forwards.

"Good luck, Cal," Yolanda said.

"Thanks," I smiled over my shoulder and went to go face this mysterious sage.

OVER MY DEAD BODY

*N*ow, I have been walking around cities my entire life. I have done many miles at a time, especially when missing the late bus from work meant either spending money on a taxi or sloughing it home. More often than not, I sloughed it. I wasn't a runner. I didn't do cross-fit. But I considered myself in reasonable shape. Certainly I could do a three hour session of yoga without falling over completely.

All that being said, climbing up that mountain left me gasping and wheezing and all around exhausted. My legs burned and I think I had pulled a muscle in my back that definitely didn't exist yesterday. I staggered to the top of the mountain—a plateau of some sort with a great view—and fell to the ground in agony. My muscles were both burning and twitching. It took me a full two minutes to catch my breath and my head was still spinning when I did. When someone handed me a glass of water, I guzzled it without thinking.

"Thanks," I said. Then froze. I turned slowly to look at the person standing next to me.

He was innocuous as far as things went. Compared to Yolanda, Thaddeus the vampire, and the wyvern, he was almost cuddly. He was almost human-looking, with fair skin and bright red hair, a pleasant expression and no obvious horns or tails or wings. I half expected him to be wearing a kilt or some such, he looked like he belonged in a movie about the highlands, but he wore an embroidered robe over fairly ordinary trousers and a shirt, instead. The edges were a bit frayed, but the embroidery was still gleaming and in one piece.

The weird thing was that the pattern was of a fish. Over and over and over again, a fish. Big, small, swimming, dying, it was the same fish.

"It's a salmon," the man said.

"Sorry, what?" I handed him back the glass of water and wondered if I was going to pay for it later. I knew from my time in a creative writing class that there were all sorts of rules about eating and drinking at various supernatural tables. I hoped this wasn't one of those situations. Then again, we were talking about salmon, so maybe it was just my imagination.

"It's a salmon," the man repeated. "The Salmon of Knowledge."

I tried to keep a straight face, I really did, but the laugh just sort of slipped out. "You've got to be kidding."

The man made an annoyed sound in the back of his throat. "No. I am not kidding."

"What in the world is a Salmon of Knowledge?" I asked, my laughs still slipping through.

"In Irish mythology, there was a salmon who swam his way into the Well of Wisdom. Into this well fell nine hazelnuts, which the salmon ate. The salmon then gained all the knowledge of the world. But the salmon was still a fish and it was caught by a poet. He knew of the salmon's knowledge and gave it to his servant to cook, so that he might gain the fish's knowledge. The servant was accidentally burned by some of the fat from the salmon and stuck his finger in his mouth. The salmon's knowledge passed instead to the servant, for the first person to eat of the fish's flesh would gain all the knowledge of the world."

"So you are..." I said.

"The servant. Fionn," he introduced himself with a flourish. I raised my eyebrows and shrugged.

"Sorry, not familiar with the tale," I said. Fionn's face grew flushed and he scowled.

"Have you never heard of the tales of Fianna? The legendary warriors?"

"No, sorry," I said. I probably shouldn't have sounded so cheerful about the fact, but the story was a bit ridiculous. I mean, really. The Salmon of Knowledge?

"What of Taliesin? Or Sigurd?" Fionn asked. Now them I had heard of. I mean, in passing, but still.

"You're them?" I sat up straighter, eager.

"No, but the principle is similar," Fionn grumbled. I deflated again. Well, there was nothing for it, I supposed. I didn't need to know who this Fionn character was to get my knowledge from him.

"Well, that's alright, I suppose. I've come to ask you a question," I said. Fionn sniffed and straightened his shoulders.

"All who find themselves on my mountain have questions," he said, adjusting his robes.

"Okay, great! So how does this work? I ask my question and we see what happens?" I said, then winced. "Those don't count as my question, by the way."

"Most of the people who come up here at least know the lore," Fionn grumbled. I got the impression that he didn't much care for me.

"Yeah, well, I'm new to this," I said. "All I got was you borrowed a troll's right hand and strangled his wife as payment."

"Interesting," Fionn murmured. "You don't look the sort to be consorting with trolls."

"You don't look the sort to strangle by proxy," I retorted. Coming to Elsewhere must have messed with my mind, because I wasn't usually this combative. Maybe it was the fact that this guy had terrified Yolanda. She was bigger than me, stronger than me and had a whole lot more knowledge about the world. But she was my assistant and I had to stick up for her. I also had to get answers to my questions or face, you know, the end of the world or some such. At the very least, my boss would be severely unimpressed with me.

Fionn wrinkled his nose as he appraised me. He stretched out his legs and leaned against an outcropping of rock that I was pretty certain hadn't been there moments ago. He looked comfortable, like he had all the time in the world. Thank goodness I hadn't upset him too badly.

"What do you wish to know?" he asked.

I considered, "You have all the knowledge of the world."

"I do. I am also bound by certain restrictions. I can only know the answer to the question you ask," Fionn said, looking at his hands absently. "I cannot answer any question that would ruin the journey for you. I cannot give you the meaning of life, because each person must figure that out for themselves."

"But if I were to ask you who killed Magnus, you could tell me?" I said.

"Is that your question? You only get one," Fionn brushed a hand over one of the salmon embroideries on his robe and fixed me with a very piercing stare. My heart started beating faster.

"Yes, alright. My question is, who killed Magnus? Life's Magnus, you know. The warrior-slash-jewel-thief that she was so fond of. Not some random Magnus." The words came out in a rush and I hoped I had made it sufficiently clear who I meant. I also really hoped I hadn't bungled the actual question. Maybe I should have come up with something more specific, like "who wants to cause an imbalance of power between Life and Death?"

Fionn glanced at me, then nodded. He opened his mouth and, before I could exclaim in surprise, bit down on his thumb. He didn't bite hard enough to sever the digit, but there was definitely blood drawn. He hissed and tossed his head back, eyes widening and pupils contracting. There weren't any bells ringing or wind blowing. It was just Fionn looking a little stunned. A moment later and he was fine, blinking off whatever had happened.

His thumb was also healed.

He turned to me, a cunning grin on his face. "Well, I have the knowledge. Now we come to matter of price."

"Shouldn't we have figured out price before the question?" I asked. I had sort of hoped that he forgot about the whole price thing. Silly human, I sighed to myself. These magical beings didn't forget that sort of thing.

"What point would there be to setting a price before I knew what the answer meant?" Fionn asked.

"Alright, how much is it going to cost me?" I winced. "I only have a few thousand in the bank and I'd have to get permission to access it and—"

"I want your life," Fionn interrupted. I choked on my words.

"Uh, what? You can't...that's not..."

"I now know how valuable this information is." Fionn examined his robes carefully. "So my price must be made accordingly. I cannot let this get out into the world. Therefore, my price is your life."

"No!" I said. "You can't kill me!"

"Very well, if you refuse my price, then I must kill you," Fionn said evenly. I felt my eyes bugging out in astonishment.

"So you were going to kill me either way?" I spluttered. "That's just not fair!"

"Life isn't fair," Fionn said with a grin.

"No," I agreed, "she isn't."

Before I could blink, the Irish sage had drawn a knife from the inside of his robes. He lunged for me. I scrabbled backwards, but I was still tired and stiff from climbing a mountain. He was fresh as a daisy and probably had some immortal powers lending him strength. He got me once on the cheek and I flinched away. I held up my arm to block Fionn's next blow, but the sage was a whole lot faster than me. He slipped past my guard and drew the blade across my throat in a death-blow.

Things went black.

Then, they weren't black.

I found myself exactly where I had been. My neck was tingling and I was very much not dead. "Holy crap!" I said.

"This is not possible!" Fionn said, driving his knife towards me again. This time, I had the good sense to roll away. While I was running from a madman with a knife, my mind was working.

I wasn't dead. I should really have been dead. My

throat had been cut—I definitely felt the knife go in all the way—and now it wasn't. I could still feel blood trickling down my cheek, so I knew I wasn't a ghost or impervious to injury. I certainly wasn't impervious to pain. So what the hell was going on?

Things clicked. Death had removed me from my life-force. That meant that I wasn't actually alive to be killed. Life had said I was immortal. I just figured that Death had kept me from ageing or disease. And, after Yolanda explained things, I figured I was just like the other immortals. Alive, but just extended, not actually immune from death. Apparently, I was wrong. I wasn't actually alive at all. Did that mean I would never die? Was I even human anymore? The thought was profoundly disturbing.

All the while my brain was puzzling this out, Fionn was still racing after me with his knife. I flopped onto my back and squealed as he bore down on me with the knife. I yelped and raised my hands in a desperate attempt to stave him off. Maybe I had just gotten lucky and he had only scratched my throat.

But on the off-chance that I wasn't lucky, "I'll pay your price!"

Fionn halted. His eyes were blazing and his skin was flushed with anger. His robes were stained red where my blood had splattered on them. "What?" he hissed.

"I'll pay your price. You can kill me and I get your answer," I said. My voice wavered. I really hoped I was making the right decision, here.

"You…but…no," Fionn said.

"You set the price. I'm willing to pay it. We have a bargain," I said. Oh, please, let me be doing this right. Fionn snarled in wordless rage and raised his knife. I screamed again, the sound high pitched and absolutely terrified. Fionn plunged his knife directly into my heart. This time, the scream was from pain.

Again, things went black. And again, they became normal. I was exactly where I was, assuredly not dead. Fionn was looking at me in disgust from a few feet away, wiping his knife on his robes. Disturbingly, the robes were dissolving my blood as though it had never been there. I think I even saw one of the salmons eat a droplet.

"You tricked me," he said.

"Honestly, I didn't," I said, sitting up.

"The price is honestly paid," Fionn spat. "But know this: if you ever set foot on my mountain again, I will use all my knowledge to find a way to tear you from this world."

Somehow, I managed to get myself standing. I felt wobbly and probably wouldn't be doing a whole lot of moving for the rest of the day, but I was in one piece. I think. "So, can I have my answer, please?"

"Very well," Fionn snapped. "Magnus was killed by an Ennedi Tiger."

My mouth dropped open, "That was what you had to kill me to protect? Are you insane?"

"Get off my mountain," Fionn raised his knife again.

"I may not be able to kill you, but I can cause you great pain."

"Right. Got it. Thanks so much. Good luck with all this," I said, backing away. As soon as my feet hit the path, I was running down it as best I could. I managed to get down the mountain in some sort of running slide that didn't tear too many of my muscles and only left me with half my skin scraped off. I felt this was a good thing compared to the alternative

I hit the end of the trail and sprinted towards Yolanda like a rabbit. She had been pacing, apparently. A small trench was worn in the soft ground where she had walked. The troll took one look at me and rushed forwards.

"Cal! Are you okay? Where are you hurt? What happened?" Yolanda asked. She patted my limbs, looking for the wound that had spouted so much blood. I pushed her away with a trembling arm.

Panting, I asked, "Yolanda, what in the world is an Ennedi Tiger?"

Yolanda took one more look at me and opened her mouth to speak. Before she got there, the day's activities and lack of oxygen rushed up to me and I fell to the ground. Yes, the great Cal Thorpe, the impossible to kill, marketing genius, the mighty human, fainted.

Sheesh.

KNOCK 'EM DEAD

I woke up in an annoyingly familiar setting. The walls were glaring white, everything hurt and I tried really hard not to scream when Graveltoes appeared too close to my face. Again. The creature blinked its enormous eyes and grinned, showing off pointed teeth.

"You are awake again!" Graveltoes exclaimed. I groaned and sat up, forcing the creature to clamber backwards. It handed me my glasses, which I cleaned thoroughly on my hospital pyjamas before slipping back on my nose.

"Why am I here?" I complained. At least this time I could talk. Sure, every bone in my body felt like it had been pulverised, but at least I could talk.

"Because you fell over," Graveltoes said as though it were obvious. I sighed.

"No, I mean why am I here and not in my house in Death's lands?" I was fairly certain that being in my really comfortable bed in a place that, while still unfamiliar, was my own, would be better than this. Almost anything would be better than waking up to Graveltoes in my face.

"Ah. Because the troll did not know what was wrong with you. She brought you here. And I did not know what was wrong with you, but you are better now, so it worked! Humans are such strange creatures to fall over like that." Graveltoes nodded sagely. I looked around and found the room empty but for the good doctor and myself.

"Where's Yolanda?" I asked, perhaps a bit pointedly. Graveltoes may have been a doctor and doing his best to heal me and make me feel better, but that didn't mean I couldn't resent him for it. And I had questions for Yolanda.

"I will go send her in," Graveltoes clambered off my bed and gave me a disapproving shake of his head. "You humans, always so impatient. Pah."

Human. Was that what I was? After being not-killed by Fionn—twice—I didn't even know if I could be considered human. Could I be killed? Was I even alive, or just stuck somewhere between Life and Death? Was I an immortal? If not, then was I something else? More? Less? Maybe most people would have been grinning widely and jumping out of airplanes at the discovery that they couldn't die. I felt more like curling up into a ball and never coming out again.

The whole point of my taking the agreement with Death was that I didn't want to die. I still had life to live and I wanted to live it. That didn't mean I wanted to be turned into some super-powerful being that would never die, even if I did still feel pain. A lot. I just wanted to live. I wanted to get my promotion and do well at my job. Heck, I even wanted to fall in love. Have a family. A life.

Death's offer had made it seem like I could at least have part of that.

But what had I lost?

"You are well." Yolanda slipped into the room and greeted me with a big smile. I nodded. The troll put my bloodied clothes on a chair. She looked at me then started fiddling with her thumbs. "I am glad you are alive."

"Am I?" I asked. "Alive? Because Fionn killed me, Yolanda. He cut my throat. Stabbed me in the heart. I should be nothing more than a corpse on his mountain."

"No." Yolanda shook her head violently. "You were separated from your life-force. You are an immortal, now!"

I scoffed. "You told me yourself that immortals can be killed. I'm pretty sure cutting my throat should have killed me. Unless, what, I'm some sort of vampire?"

"You are human," Yolanda said. She paused and took a shaky breath. "But you are right. You are not alive. The transition that bound you to Death must have been different because you are human, making you impossible to kill."

"So I *am* some sort of vampire or zombie or whatever," I said. Bile rose in the back of my throat and for a second, the room spun.

"No," Yolanda said. "Vampires may not be dead, but they are not undead. It's complicated. They...they're bound to the blood. They take on the life-force of other beings through their blood. This gives them life. They are technically alive, though they had to die first to become as they are."

"Right, that makes no sense at all," I said. I was happy to accept that I wasn't a vampire. I wasn't feeling any weird urges to drink blood, so that must mean I was alright. Right? "So I'm some sort of zombie?"

Yolanda actually snorted in derision at that. "Zombies are animated corpses. They have no connection to either Life or Death because they are held together by pure magic. They do not think or experience. They only do what they are told."

I tugged at the sheets on the bed. "So then what am *I*?"

"Human," Yolanda replied firmly. I frowned. "It is the truth. You were separated from your life-force, therefore you are not alive. But because you are bound to Death, you cannot die as such until he either releases you or is killed himself. Which won't happen."

I choked quietly at Yolanda's words. Something in my chest tightened and wouldn't let me breathe. I felt tears gathering in my eyes and looked away from my assistant.

"Most would be revelling in their new power,"

Yolanda said, sounding confused. I took off my glasses and blinked furiously while pretending to clean them.

"I never wanted immortality," I said. "I just wanted a nice life."

"But you shook Death's hand! You made the bargain for this. This escape from dying. For immortality," Yolanda said. There was an edge to her voice, like if I was rejecting this, I was rejecting her. I couldn't stop the hurt and the panic, though.

"I didn't think it through," I managed to whisper. My throat closed and all that escaped me were sobs that shook my shoulders.

"You are still human, Cal," Yolanda said, voice soft. Comforting. She lay a hand on my arm. "Don't forget that. So what if you can't be killed. At least you still have your humanity."

"And what is humanity if not being short lived enough that we must appreciate what we do have? And you know what? I didn't do that. I never realised what I had and what I actually wanted. Now it's gone," I snarled. "Life told me so herself. I was never a warrior. I never fought for life. I just...gave it up."

"You're not dead, Cal," Yolanda said firmly. "And you are still human."

"Yeah. Sure. I'm not alive, but I can't die," I said. I shook my head and decided to change the subject. It wasn't going to help either of us to argue over something that was impossible to change, or to comprehend. My very existence was in question and I doubted that Yolanda had the answers I sought. I couldn't just lie here and sulk, either. Not when I still had work to do. I stretched and felt my muscles complain loudly in protest. "Why does everything still hurt?"

Yolanda shrugged, relief flickering through her eyes. "This I do not know. A part of your humanity? You still feel hunger and thirst, so why should you not feel pain? Everyone has limits they must adhere to."

"That is not encouraging at all," I grumbled. The sarcasm and good-natured cynicism was a lie, a facade, and it hurt to wear. "Am I going to grow old? Get sick?"

"I don't know," Yolanda said. "My knowledge of the situation is very limited. Humans are…strange. I only know what Death told me and what I have experienced of his powers. You could ask him."

"And he'll give me another one of those not-quite answers that got me into this whole situation," I said. "I should have just taken the bullet. It would have been far less work."

"But not nearly as much fun, right?" Yolanda smiled, flashing her white teeth at me. I gaped at her.

"Seriously? You think this is fun? You, the one who is scared of your own shadow, not to mention every being we've encountered. Including the guy you work for, by the way." I sat up a bit more and winced at the pain. This was really, really bizarre.

"But you are not dead and we have some information, no?" Yolanda clapped her big hands together and looked at me eagerly.

"Um, right. The, ah…Ennedi Tiger," I said, pinching the bridge of my nose. "I've never heard of it, but Fionn seemed to think that it was important enough to kill me over."

I explained what happened on the top of the mountain and Yolanda nodded, looking serious. "Yes, it is bad."

"I don't even know what this tiger-thing is," I said. "Can it be that dangerous, trying to pit Death against Life and changing the balance of the world and what not?"

"The Ennedi Tiger is not the one seeking to destroy the balance," Yolanda said. "It is just a beast. Dangerous, but of no great intellect."

"Seriously?" I complained. "I went all the way up to that mountain and got attacked by a bitter has-been and all I got out of it was the *murder weapon?*"

"No, you do not understand," Yolanda said, still sounding annoyingly eager. "The Ennedi Tiger is a sacred being of the Order of Silence!"

For a moment, her words meant nothing to me. I closed my eyes and tried to think, then jerked forwards. "Wait. The Order of Silence? Like the people that Mercy work for? The *assassin?!*"

"Yes," Yolanda agreed with a broad smile. "We will go talk to them!"

"Hold on," I said, shaking my head. "Shouldn't you be, I don't know, quaking in terror at the prospect? You nearly had a panic attack when Mercy showed up at the office, and that was just to get information on what Death is like. I'm pretty sure that invading their stronghold and demanding to know why they had Life's warrior was killed is going to be a whole lot worse than that."

Yolanda frowned and shook her head. "You do not know anything, do you?"

"No, not about this, I don't," I snapped.

"We will make an appointment," Yolanda said slowly, as though I were a child. I shot her a look. "The Order of Silence is bound to do no harm when you make an appointment. We will be there in an official capacity."

"Seriously?" I asked. "These people are bound by the sacred nature of appointments?"

Yolanda nodded, smiling again. She handed me a clean set of clothes and I took them. Reluctantly. "You dress, we will go. It will be good." She tromped out of the room, the ground shaking slightly in her eagerness. I looked at the black slacks and black t-shirt. They were in my size, but was the "I work for Death" vibe really necessary?

I sighed and climbed slowly out of the bed, my muscles still sore but slightly less painful. Still, it took me far longer than it should have to dress, and when I did, I couldn't help but glance at my subtle reflection in the mirror. I still had a cut on my cheek and some of the bruises had risen to great purple splotches. I looked terrible.

"Right, well, you'll have to work on your image later," I told my marketing-conscious self. "Because you're off to the sacred land of lawyers. Assassin lawyers. Goodie."

I huffed at myself and shuffled to the door. Somehow, I managed to get down to the street. I half-expected Iggie—because, really, I couldn't remember his name—to be waiting with the Rolls. Instead, I looked around and found an empty street. No Yolanda, no Iggie, no nothing.

I looked around, the hair on the back of my neck prickling. I spotted a cobbled side street beside a tudor-style house and wandered in that direction, wondering if maybe Yolanda had just gotten tired of waiting and went for a coffee. Instead, I found the troll standing stock still, her arms pinned to her side by some sort of mysterious force, her eyes wide and her mouth forced shut. She struggled against whatever was holding her in place and stared at me pointedly. I got the message loud and clear: run.

Maybe if I were more heroic, I would have stayed and done my best to fight off whatever was holding my assistant. But I had no special skills to fight anything and even though I was immune to death, that didn't mean I couldn't be hurt. A lot. And I was fairly certain that I wouldn't be any help to Yolanda if I stayed. Not to mention that whatever was going on, she wasn't being hurt. She was being held. Logic told me that she wasn't the target, I was.

So I did the only thing I knew how to do. I ran.

I didn't get very far. Almost as soon as I emerged onto the street, a shadow solidified in front of me. A moment later, two more surrounded me. I turned, looking for a way out, and found nothing. The shadow took form and I found myself facing Thaddeus, Prince of the House of Vampyr.

He was dressed in a very expensive but sloppy pair of slacks and grey shirt. He still had his hat to protect him from the sun and his hair stuck out at odd angles. The vampire grinned at me, flashing his over-long canines. "Cal Thorpe! It is so good to see you again!"

"Uh, hi, Thaddeus," I said. "Look, I'm a little busy. I haven't had the opportunity to talk to Death about your proposal..."

"No matter," Thaddeus said, taking a step forwards. I instinctively backed up and found myself being held by an equally-pretty and unkempt female vampire with blonde hair that was frizzy as I'll get out in a dress in a garish shade of purple. "We've decided this is too important to leave until later."

"Now hold on a minute, you can't just—" I started to protest, doing my best to pull away. The vampiress was exceptionally strong, though. And her smile was really quite creepy.

"Oh, but I can," Thaddeus' pleasant smile turned a bit brittle. He nodded sharply to the other vampire and in a second, we were nothing but smoke and shadow.

I screamed. At least, I thought I was screaming, but there was very little air and I couldn't hear anything. I thought I saw features passing us by—a shape that looked like a tree, possibly a house or two—but everything moved too quickly for me to be sure. After what felt like ages, we solidified again.

I staggered around, trying to gain control of my feet. My brain and my stomach moved at different times and I barely managed to make it to a planter before emptying my stomach. I groaned and clutched at my stomach. "Seriously, let's never do that again," I said.

"You will become better equipped to handle such things," Thaddeus said, his voice terrifyingly close. I jumped and my still-spinning brain couldn't move fast enough to catch my balance. I fell over, nearly knocking myself on the head. Thaddeus tsked, drawing my attention.

What *also* drew my attention was the enormous castle behind him. Okay, having been to Life's palatial mansion and Death's manor, you would think maybe I'm being a bit judicious in my use of the word. But seriously. It was a castle. A gothic castle straight out of Eastern Europe, complete with stones bigger than a standing man, towers and turrets, and walls for soldiers to stand on.

We were standing in a courtyard that came straight out of a film. I mean, really, what castle actually had a bubbling fountain in the centre, let alone perfectly sculpted hedges in planters, sculptures of prancing unicorns and romantic trellises with roses? I had figured Thaddeus to be a little obsessed with image, but this was ridiculous.

"Welcome to House Vampyr," Thaddeus spread his arms wide and did a little bow. The other vampires that he had brought with him crowded close. The female peered closely at me and I crawled backwards away from her. She licked her lips.

"Can I have a taste, Highness?" she asked, voice deep and throaty. "Just a little one?"

"No!" Thaddeus' voice whipped out and I saw the female flinch away. She cowered a little at Thaddeus' feet, whimpering. "No. Cal is far too valuable for that. He is going to help us refine our image."

"Seriously, this is *not* the time," I said, clambering to my feet. "Death is going to be mighty peeved that you—"

"Death is too busy with his marital troubles," Thaddeus waved his hand dismissively. "Besides, why would he bother with a human like you? No, *we* appreciate your skills far more than he ever would. We have already started implementing your suggestions!"

Thaddeus grabbed my hand and dragged me along behind him. I stumbled. His superhuman strength and determination kept me from falling completely on my face. I was pulled into a side yard full of vibrant grass and blossoming cherry trees where four people were sitting behind easels. Before the easels stood four vampires, all holding some sort of ridiculous pose, all looking rather the worse for wear. It wasn't the vampires that startled me, though, it was the artists. They were bleeding.

There were various puncture marks on the side of the artists' necks and from what I could tell, the blood wasn't clotting. I saw one girl's hand shaking so badly that she could hardly draw a straight line.

"What are you doing?!" I cried.

"We got artists to draw our pictures," Thaddeus said as if it were obvious. "We found them in a beautiful little art institute in Florence. I love Florence."

"They're bleeding!" I gestured to the man closest to me, who was breathing heavily.

"I know," Thaddeus said in distaste. At least, I thought it was distaste. His nostrils were flaring and I could see his pupils dilating in pure desire. "It is sometimes necessary. They were not cooperating. We had to bleed them a little to make them more compliant."

I don't remember much from the Dracula book I read in high school English, but I did remember that being fed upon by a vampire was bad news. It made you addicted. You craved it. And they grew stronger while you suffered and died. And maybe became one of them. I had to get these artists out of here or they were going to die.

And they were still the breakable, killable sort of human.

"Let them go," I snapped.

"Why?" Thaddeus chuckled. "It was your suggestion."

"I suggested you *hire* an artist! For *money*! Not coerce them into working for you. You can't just take people from their lives and force them to paint your portrait," I said, more than a little desperate. One of the artists looked at me with a flick of his eyes. He whimpered, but a hiss from the vampire he was painting forced his attention back to his work. "I mean, that's just slavery, plain and simple!"

Thaddeus looked at me for a moment, his mouth splitting into a wide grin. "You really are that naïve, aren't you?"

I took a step back.

"We're predators, Cal, that's what we do," Thaddeus smirked. "I mean, really. What did you expect we did? Live on tomato juice and steak? We are *hunters*. And we hunt humans. These artists have a particular skill, or they wouldn't be alive, here in the centre of House Vampyr. They're the lucky ones."

I took another step back, my hand brushing a stone wall behind me. "You're keeping them as slaves, though! And you've addicted them to whatever it is you do. How can any of that be useful? It's the worst marketing ploy I've ever seen!"

"It does lower their life expectancy, but what is a few more days when all humans are so short lived?" Thaddeus rolled his eyes at the inconvenience. Anger flared in me and I balled my fists at my side.

"Let them go," I snarled. "Or...or you'll never get me to do any marketing for you."

Thaddeus just laughed at that. One of those annoying, two note, mocking laughs, too. He looked at me like I was an idiot. I really wanted to knock his hat off and see what happened when he got a taste of the sun. I also really wanted to run away. But I wasn't going to do either. I needed to get those artists out of there.

"Cal, I had hoped we could do this without any

undue…difficulty," Thaddeus shook his head, putting his hand over his heart. "But you're being uncooperative."

I started to throw back snark at him when Thaddeus surged forwards. He moved faster than I could track him, becoming nothing more than a blur in my eyes. I felt something slam into my throat and then I was being pushed back until I hit the wall. Thaddeus stood there, his hand grasping my throat tight enough to make me see spots. I gasped, but nothing came out. My lungs started burning and the spots grew bigger.

Then, surprise surprise, Thaddeus drew back his lips and sank his fangs into my neck. The first sensation was one of panic. Then there was almost no sensation at all. It was like floating. It wasn't unpleasant, but it wasn't pleasant either. It just sort of was. I didn't feel like I was going to be addicted to whatever this was. At least I couldn't die from it, I supposed. I just had to wait until he figured that out.

Thaddeus pulled back from me with a cry. He blurred until he was standing nearly twenty feet away. His mouth was covered in my blood and his eyes were wide with shock. "What…what is *wrong* with you?" he breathed. I frowned, confused. Then Thaddeus began to cough. With each cough, his already pale skin moved more towards pallid, then grey. He started wheezing and gagging. I could see the desperation in his eyes when he lunged for me again. Before he could get anywhere near me, Thaddeus crumbled to dust.

The vampires in the small courtyard started

screaming. The sound was like a pack of very large predators doing their best to tell everyone to stay far, far away. The vampires spontaneously turned into smoke or ran as far from me as possible.

I leaned back against the wall, trying to control the shaking in my legs. The artists all turned to look at me like they were coming out of a drug-haze. I saw the young girl blink a few times and frown deeply. "Well, hi," I said, trying to sound friendly and non-threatening. "I'm Cal Thorpe. PR agent for…you probably don't need to know this. How do we get you back to Florence?"

UNDER PAIN OF DEATH

I barely had a chance to take a step towards the poor artists—who were just beginning to realise how badly they were bleeding—before the grassy yard became crowded with people. Well, vampires. These were armed to the teeth, even beyond their own fangs. They wore armour and some had swords belted at their waist, while others pointed spears. Of all the vampires I had met thus far, these ones actually looked like they knew what they were about. They didn't seem to be worried about their clothes clashing with their skin, be it pale or dark. They just wielded weapons with a practised, deadly grace. They looked wildly around before settling on me, the only human not bleeding, though I think some smears from Thaddeus' pitiful feeding remained. The artists just blinked and looked dazed, though I could see one of them start to blink and squint at the world around her.

"Don't move," the leader of this very impressive ragtag guard hissed at me. A spear settled beneath my throat and I held up my hands. The vampire holding the spear pressed it closer to me. "What happened?"

One of the vampire females that had been posing for a portrait pointed an accusing finger at me. "He killed Prince Thaddeus!"

The leader turned to me, teeth bared. "Is this true?"

"In my defence, he did try to feed on me," I said. "I said this was a bad time, but he didn't listen."

"Your attitude will not help you here," the guard growled. I shrugged and received a jab at my shoulder from the spear in response. Ow. I looked down and saw a small trickle of blood running down my sweater. At this rate, I was going through clothes faster than any teenager. "Move, human."

I didn't ask where I was being taken. Wherever it was, it wasn't going to be good. And I couldn't even keep an eye on the artists. They were herded into the group of guards behind me. I tried to turn and see what was happening, but received another jab for my efforts.

I was corralled through the courtyards and into the castle proper. As I passed through the enormous walls of stone, something in me withered a bit. Fear started gnawing at the pit of my stomach. These walls were built to keep enemies out and people in. They were not designed for average humans to escape. If we became trapped here, then very little would get us out. Then the massive wooden doors closed behind us and that fear started writing in earnest.

The weird part was that I wasn't afraid for me. The vampires could kill me—or try—but there would be no lasting damage. They could torture me, and I'm fairly certain I would start weeping like a child within minutes, but I had walked into this situation with my eyes open. Sort of. I was fairly certain that Death would come for me eventually, once Life started getting really angry. And if not, then I would probably end up insane, which didn't sound particularly pleasant but could be worse. Still, I had a better chance of understanding what I was doing than the artists did. It was my fault that they were here, my stupid suggestion that had Thaddeus kidnapping humans and enthralling them into working for him. And they were a lot more breakable than I was.

The guard spread around a massive room until it was just me standing in the centre, the four other humans sort of cowering a distance behind me. Whatever conditioning had happened to them was wearing off and panic was setting in.

I stood as calmly as I could, trying to exude confidence and prove that the others could trust me. I don't think it worked. The lead guard still had a spear to my back, marching me forwards. The room we were in was not meant to be confidence-inducing.

The stone walls were oppressive and dark, despite being meticulously clean. The floor sloped gently upwards to a dais, where a stunning and inhuman beauty sat on a chair. She had the sort of looks that would have been average had they not been so perfectly appealing. Her dark hair was pulled back and she wore a red gown shot through with gold. It reminded me of those ones that you saw in pictures of Marie Antoinette. Ridiculous and opulent and somehow intimidating.

The one thing that was a bit weird was that the vamipress had not a single hair out of place. There was none of that scruffy, not-quite put-together look that everyone else had. She was perfectly sculpted. And all the more inhuman for it. My heart started beating a touch faster.

"*You* were the one who killed the prince?" she asked, lifting her chin. I was shoved forwards by the point of the spear.

"It wasn't intentional," I defended, turning enough to glare at the guard. "Thaddeus—"

"*Prince* Thaddeus!" the woman demanded, tightening her grip on the arms of her chair so that the stone creaked. I swallowed, that fear in my belly rearing its head.

"Prince Thaddeus," I corrected, "tried to feed from me."

"Tried? He obviously succeeded, or you would not have the puncture marks on your neck," the woman hissed.

"Well, with all due respect, ah, ma'am," I tried to explain. My ignorance got me yet-another stab with the tip of the spear. I flinched and tried to ignore the fact that my back was feeling quite warm and sticky.

"Her Majesty Queen Alsatia, of House Vampyr," the guard snarled at me. Alsatia, seriously? Like an Alsatian dog? They were what people called German Shepherds for ages in Europe. I had done a marketing campaign for a dog breeder to the celebrities and learned all sorts of trivia about dogs. The image of a dog in a dress flashed into my head and I quickly covered my snicker by coughing into my hand. That thought wasn't going to help my cause at all, so I kept it to myself.

"Right, Your Majesty," I bowed slightly at the waist. "Prince Thaddeus did actually start to feed on me. He was trying to, ah...ensure my compliance."

"And why would my grandson bother with you?" the queen asked, disdain practically dripping from her voice.

"Because I'm a marketing agent? I work for Death—"

This was startling enough to have Queen Alsatia rise from her seat in a swift rush of wind. She stared at me with mouth wide open. Okay, yes, I know I wasn't all that much to look at what with the not-quite athletic physique and glasses and average hair and looks and what-not, but surely an employee of Death could look like anything? I mean, look at Yolanda! I wouldn't have thought she would be an employee of Death. Justice and Mercy, sure. But—

"You are a marketing agent?" the queen breathed, eyes wide.

Oh. Right.

"Yes," I said. "I work for Death. His PR manager and image consultant. As a matter of fact, I was running an errand for him when Prince Thaddeus kidnapped me and—"

"And with good reason!" Queen Alsatia watched me and I was fairly certain that she would start drooling at any second.

"Anyways," I said more forcefully, "I tried explaining to Prince Thaddeus that I was busy, but he wouldn't listen and so he tried to make me compliant."

"Fool!" Alsatia hissed through her teeth. Finally, some sympathy. "You are far too valuable to ruin in such a manner!"

"You people have some seriously messed up priorities!" I said. I think the guard would have happily stabbed me deeply for that, but at learning my profession even he was treating me deferentially. "You do realise that because your Prince Thaddeus tried to feed on me, that he just turned into dust?"

"Yes," Alsatia drew the word out in distaste. "And it is an unfortunate accident—"

"What is *wrong* with you?!" I demanded. "You're more worried about my marketing skills than the fact that your grandson is dead!"

"Is that a confession of murder?" Alsatia took a step forwards to the edge of the dais.

"What? No! It was an accident," I said, raising my hands. "I didn't mean to kill him. He just...I think it has something to do with my working for Death. And—"

"As long as we don't feed on you, then we are safe," Alsatia asked, but I got the impression it wasn't really a question. She looked slowly around the room and settled her gaze on the artists. Her tongue darted out to lick her lips, faster than anything normal. "But they do not work for Death."

"Now hold on just a minute," I protested, stepping back so I stood in front of the artists. I got nowhere with my protest.

"Take the food to the pens. Take our honoured guest to the dungeons," Alsatia waved a hand imperiously. "I shall enjoy talking with him about...image."

The guards around the room surged forwards with their weapons drawn. The youngest artist, a girl who still had her hair in braids, let out a piteous scream and collapsed against an older gentleman. The four artists huddled tightly together, hoping that somehow they would be spared. Or maybe they were just hoping for a little comfort in the last moments of their lives.

"No!" I cried out and did my best to get to the artists. Maybe I could demand that they be put under my protection. Or maybe I could hire them as temps for Death and some of my protection would rub off on them. Instead, I found my arms pinned to my sides by someone far stronger than any human. The artists were surrounded and the girl let out a whimper. Too scared to scream properly.

"No," I breathed desperately. I had to reach them. I had to do something!

Then, just as the artists were being dragged to a side door, there was a booming thunder. The great wooden doors that closed us off from the outside world shook. There was more thunder and each rolling sound was preceded by the shaking of the doors. After six or so of these booms, the doors started to crack.

Something wanted to get in. And it was succeeding.

"Guards!" Alsatia commanded, her voice like iron. The guards gave up on the artists and fell into rank. The vampire holding my arms released me to fill in a gap in the defences. I ran to where the other humans huddled, eyes wide and frightened. They shrank together even more as I approached. I knelt before them, trying to smile encouragingly.

"We're going to get out of here," I whispered. One of the men, a youngish sort with a beard that needed desperate trimming, furrowed his brows.

"Or we will die," he said in a thick accent. Eastern European, maybe. Maybe Russian. Either way, it wasn't helpful.

"That's not helpful," I told him. I rubbernecked around to look around for a way to get out of this room—and came up with two options which were both guarded fiercely—when the door splintered to pieces.

The light from outside streamed in. It wasn't sunlight, by any means, but the vampires hissed and shifted. Or maybe they were reacting to the shadow standing in the middle of the doorway. The shadow had hulking shoulders, massive muscles, hands balled into fists. It was the better part of twelve feet tall and it let out a bellow that rattled the stones of the castle. Best of all, I recognised her.

The vampires surged forwards. Like their counterpart in Stoker's books, they were fast. And strong. Some of them flickered into shadow and mist before appearing behind Yolanda and attacking her. She was surrounded on all sides and was going up against beings that designed to be the predator for humans. But Yolanda wasn't human. She was a rock troll.

The spears couldn't cut her thick skin. They had to be directly stabbed to make any sort of difference and that required standing still for more than a second. Yolanda did her best to crush anyone who was that foolish. She backhanded the leader of the guards who had poked holes into me and he flew to the wall, landing with a sickening crunch. The other guards hesitated, which gave Yolanda the opportunity to step on them or, in one instant, tear the arms off of a struggling vampire.

The battle seemed to be favouring Yolanda. The only problem was that she was fighting a bunch of not-dead weaponised predators. The leader got back up and headed straight for her, swiping his spear across the tendon on the back of Yolanda's right ankle. She roared and wrapped her hand around his head, squeezing until there was nothing left.

I threw up in the corner. Two of the artists did the same. The others just cowered, their eyes wide and their jaws working to produce soundless screams.

Once I got my stomach under control, I realised

Yolanda couldn't keep this up. That cut had done some serious damage. She wasn't able to move nearly as swiftly and even the little pricks from spears and swords were adding up. The vampires were gaining the upper hand. They were getting close enough to start using their fangs and claws, which were decidedly more dangerous. That meant that I had to do something.

I looked around and saw Alsatia standing before her throne, expression twisted in annoyance. I shifted and felt a stab of pain in my wounded shoulder. My thoughts somehow managed to solidify into a potentially not-stupid idea. I pushed hard at the wound in my shoulder and nearly blacked out from the pain. But I was bleeding again. I collected a few drops of blood in my cupped hand. Then, I ran for all I was worth towards Alsatia.

The queen flicked her eyes to me and ignored me. I wasn't much of a threat against a full-blown vampire. The rampaging troll, on the other hand? A serious threat.

That gave me the opportunity to get behind the vampire and wrap a hand under her chin, forcing her mouth up. I tilted my other hand so the blood was an instant from dropping into her mouth.

"Everybody stop!" I yelled. Even through the sounds of the fight, my voice echoed loudly enough to draw the attention of the fighting forces. The vampires stiffened and started rushing towards me. Yolanda hit a couple of them hard enough that they stopped, twitching on the floor.

"Nobody do anything, or I pour my blood down your queen's throat. And we all saw how well that worked for Prince Thaddeus," I said. Alsatia was smart enough not to struggle, though we both knew how much stronger than me she was. The other vampires seemed torn between flying off the handle in anger and doing what I said. Luckily for me, they were smart enough that they kept still.

"What do you want, human?" Alsatia asked, doing her best not to move as she spoke.

"First off, you're going to let all the humans go. The artists, I mean," I said. "You will release them into the custody of the troll. And I'm going to go with them. You're going to let us go and leave your land. No sneaky attempts to try and kill us."

"What's to stop me from killing you as soon as you move away?" Alsatia snarled.

"Honestly, you can do whatever you want," I replied, tilting my hand a touch more. "But I'm not sure you would like the result of that. And Death wouldn't be too pleased with you killing his marketing agent. Not to mention twelve feet of angry troll."

Alsatia was quiet for a moment. "Very well," she spat.

"Get her to promise on the earth of her homeland," Yolanda rumbled, her voice much deeper than usual. I nudged Alsatia.

"You heard her," I said. "By the earth of your homeland."

Alsatia let out a sound of rage and I saw her features twist. I understood, suddenly, why people used to think that vampires were malevolent demons, ugly and terrible. They might have learned how to blend in with the human population since then—sort of—but they were still terrible beings that fed on the life blood of others.

Popular media had a lot to apologise for.

"Very well. I swear by the earth of my homeland that you, your troll, and the food will have safe passage through my lands," Alsatia spat. I looked at Yolanda, who nodded. I pulled my hand away from Alsatia and stepped aside. I wiped the excess blood on my already-ruined shirt.

"Works for me," I said. I walked up to Yolanda, passing by all those really-angry vampires. They stood there and did nothing, just glared at me with a good deal of malice.

The artists had already pressed closer to the door. Yolanda helped me usher them outside and we walked in silence for a bit until we were well-away from the castle. The sun shining down on us helped dispel the fear that we would be followed, that the vampires would ignore their queen and hunt us down. We followed a dirt path through a meadow that looked like it had come straight out of one of those historical movies. The artists were trembling, though from relief or fear, I didn't know. I understood completely.

"So, you're a bit taller than I remember," I told

Yolanda, who was indeed towering over me a lot more than usual. Actually, it looked like she had done weightlifting on serious steroids. Even her teeth gleamed more than usual, almost blinding when they caught the full sun.

"Troll battle magic," she explained. "It will wear off in about an hour."

"Great. Because I might get neck strain trying to look up at you all the time," I said. Yolanda grinned and let out a basso laugh. I was so relieved not to be prisoners of those vampires, all humans free and not-dead, that I laughed, too. The artists let out frightened squeaks, but they continued to follow along behind us, their hands all clasped together.

I told Yolanda what had happened with Thaddeus and why she had, therefore, charged into a full-blown execution scene. She tilted her head and considered. "You are not connected to life-force. Vampires feed on others' life forces. That could be why he, well, poofed."

"But shouldn't he have just not been able to get sustenance out of me? I mean, why poof? I mean, does it have something to do with my connection to Death? Like, instead of a life-force, I have a death force or something? I think I'm going to have to make a list of things to ask Death, and *not* about his marketing campaign. Ah, well, it doesn't matter right now. The real question is, how in the world are we going to get them back to Florence?" I gestured to the artists walking in front of us. The girl tripped and fell into the arms of the accented man. She smiled up at him and I just shook my head.

Humans. Go through being kidnapped by vampires for the purpose of drawing their portraits, almost get killed by violent and bloody means, survive a rampaging battle, and what matters? Whether the guy caught you when you tripped.

We are such a strange species.

olanda and I settled in a small tavern somewhere just beyond the border of the vampire territory. The tavern seemed a little convenient, the biggest building in a tiny village sitting at a crossroads just beyond the border. It was surprisingly well populated, though, with creatures of all sorts drinking and eating and making a serious racket. Yolanda said that the denizens of Elsewhere enjoyed two things almost as much as they enjoyed gathering power and causing trouble: alcohol and caffeine. As a result, there were almost as many cafes and taverns—not bars, mind you—per capita as any of the major cities in the mortal realm. This, oddly, made me feel a whole lot better about things.

Yolanda left me at the tavern, saying that she would deal with the artists—this, apparently, included a memory modifier. She handed me two gold coins for my food and drink and I happily left her to deal with the unfortunate humans caught up in this mess. I don't know how she managed to get the artists back to Florence, but when she came in to sit next to me, they were gone.

"Want something to eat?" I asked, lifting my hand to call over the barkeep. She was some sort of gargoyle-type creature, with large bat ears, a visage of stone and long, deadly claws. Yolanda ordered eagerly and I took a long sip of my...I think it was mead. The drink went down smoothly and I felt the slight release of tension that the alcohol gave.

"Where did they go?" I asked. Yolanda shifted in the seat and shrank a few inches. She was almost back at normal size and she looked particularly tired, covering up at least two yawns in the space of a few seconds. I guess battle magic isn't for the faint hearted or the under-caffeinated.

"There are not all that many ways to the mortal realms," Yolanda said. "I had to whistle up a Ferryman."

"A Ferryman," I said blankly.

"Ferrier of souls from the land of the living to the land of the dead, wherever the souls go," Yolanda explained. "Or, in this case, from Elsewhere to Florence."

I took another pull of my mead, feeling oddly calm about having sent four humans with a rock troll to go meet a Ferrier of souls to the land of the dead. I had other worries to consider. "This place just gets weirder and weirder."

The gargoyle barkeep set down two large plates of

brisket before Yolanda and myself. My assistant dug in gladly, scarfing the food faster than some dogs. I watched, picking at my own food with a fork.

After a few minutes, Yolanda looked up at me, sauce smeared all over her face. She frowned. "You seem… sad? Where your face gets all pinched and worried?"

"Sad," I confirmed. I leaned back in my chair, staring at the wooden whorls of the table. "I killed someone."

"You mean the vampire."

"Yeah," I kept my eyes on the table. "And not an hour later, I was laughing."

"You did not kill him," Yolanda said firmly. I looked at her in pure surprise. She held out her hands. "Truly. He was the one who fed on you. He tried to bind you to his will. And neither he—nor you—knew what would happen. He died, but it wasn't your fault."

"He still died because of me," I said. My throat suddenly felt very tight; I didn't think I could eat any more of the brisket.

"Yes," Yolanda agreed. "But that does not make it your fault."

I said nothing. I knew that what she was saying was the truth. There was nothing I could have done. I couldn't change things. That didn't mean the guilt was going to go away. The whole situation had been my fault. Maybe that was why I was so glad to have left Yolanda to send the artists back to Florence. I had suggested to Thaddeus that they use human artists to paint portraits, in order to increase social media views.

I mean, I hadn't known what the consequences would be, but perhaps I should have. Everything I had learned in the mortal world about vampires—no matter how far fetched—agreed on one thing: they were predators, killers. Telling someone back home how to increase their social media hits would have done very little. Here, it nearly cost four people their lives, and killed one other.

"Did you know that all vampires used to be human?" Yolanda asked after a moment.

My stomach dropped to my feet and I pushed the plate of brisket away. Yolanda grabbed it and ate without asking. I didn't begrudge it to her at all. "I thought they were demons. Possessed corpses or something."

"Vampirism, like a cold, is a disease. Or a virus. Whichever," Yolanda said between forkfuls. "It only affects humans. It is also only spread by contact with bodily fluids. Blood, primarily."

"So, what, under their pretty facade, they're just diseased humans? I saw the queen's face change when I had her pinned." I clenched my hand where I had held my blood. If what Yolanda said was true, then I had not only killed someone, but threatened a human. Not an undead monster.

"Are there no diseases that change your appearance? That make you less human, less what you were? Where the disease takes control of you and your actions?" Yolanda asked. She finished off my own lunch and pushed that plate away, too. "They are diseased. The blood they take feeds the disease, making it stronger. Until the human parts are pushed so far aside that it is only the disease talking."

I swallowed down bile. "I think you're talking about a parasite," I breathed. "A foreign entity that uses a body as its host in order to live and propagate and survive. Malevolent. Controlling."

Yolanda waved a dismissive hand, "Disease, parasite. One is smaller, the other bigger. It matters not. Vampirism destroys all that they were until they are literally nothing more than slaves to their drive for blood. The human mind, gone. The human soul, gone. All that remains is the disease."

"So, what, you're saying what I did to Thaddeus was a mercy?" I snapped. Yolanda blinked her large yellow eyes at me, a faint smile touching her mouth.

"It is no accident that Mercy is an assassin," she said softly.

I sat back in my chair like she had physically hit me. I didn't know what to say to that. How to react. I felt anger, pain, guilt, relief, a myriad of emotions that I couldn't easily sort through. My throat grew tight again and I bit my lip to keep from letting the hysterical sobs out. I clenched my fists in my lap to keep from hitting the table.

The gargoyle barkeep came by to collect our plates. Yolanda paid for her meal and drink with another couple of coins and we were left in peace again. Peace being a relative term. I didn't say anything. Yolanda didn't seem terribly inclined to say anything, either. So we sat there for a while, me trying to process everything and failing miserably. That left only one thing to do: get back to work. My problems paled in comparison to what would happen if Yolanda and I didn't figure out what had happened to Magnus—that could potentially mean the end of the world.

"Can we still get an appointment with the Order of Silence?" I asked quietly after I couldn't stand hearing my own thoughts anymore. Yolanda nodded.

"We will have to clean up," she said, gesturing to my bloody shirt and her torn and ripped jeans and shirt. "The Order has strict protocol regarding appointments."

"Is there any chance of getting some sleep in there?" I asked. I might have had a chance to be unconscious, but there was nothing about it that had given me a rest. Coupled with dealing with a horde of angry vampires, I was beginning to feel the day. Not to mention Yolanda must be tired. I had no idea what battle magic took out of a person, but given how much she had eaten, I doubted that she was any less tired than me. I could have been completely wrong, though. I had no idea how much trolls ate on a daily basis.

Yolanda shook her head, pushing back from the table with a clatter of wood. The patrons looked at us for a brief moment before apparently deciding that we were beneath their interest and getting back to their drinking and dining. "The longer we take to get this situation resolved, the worse the imbalance will grow."

"Really? How can you tell?" I followed her out of the

tavern and we trudged towards the closest wyvern station.

"Someone is running around with the power to cause death without Death being the wiser," Yolanda said flatly. "How could the imbalance not grow larger?"

"Ah."

She stopped at a clothing store two fronts down from the tavern. We ducked inside and she made a purchase from what looked like an elf. And not a Tolkien-style elf. This looked more like your friendly Christmas elf, minus the pointed teeth. One of these days, I was going to have Yolanda take me on a creature-identifying tour. I didn't want to accidentally offend someone for misidentifying them. I doubted that all my limbs would remain intact if I didn't learn quickly.

Yolanda handed me a clean sweater and I pulled off my old shirt. Some of the fabric caught in my wounds and I whimpered. "I have been injured more in the last two days than I have in my entire life," I complained as I pulled the sweater over my injuries, trying not to start them bleeding again. The Order would just have to deal with it. "I mean, I never even broke a bone before this!"

"You have a broken bone now?" Yolanda asked. She had changed faster than I did. And it was a strange sight indeed to find Yolanda in a dress. Her bulk made the fabric stretch and I finally realised that, troll though Yolanda might be, she was also pure muscle. It was like looking at one of those pictures of female body-builders, except this one was built more like a brick wall and had a whole lot more power. And grey skin with no hair. Anyways. The dress was a medieval gown and kirtle style and Yolanda had a belt around her thick waist. I was surprised to find that it didn't actually look bad. I shouldn't be so harsh on my assistant, I supposed.

"No," I shook my head and tried to figure out where to put my old sweater. Yolanda handed it to the elf-thing, who glared and muttered something unkind under its breath. "I was just saying that as an example."

"You cannot be killed. I would think a few cuts and bruises would be negligible in comparison," Yolanda said. We left the shop and headed towards the wyvern station. I grumbled.

"It still hurts," I said. "Hey, wait a minute, isn't the wyvern that way? Where are we going?"

"The Order of Silence cannot be reached by wyvern," Yolanda said. I tried to ignore how happy she sounded about that. She nodded her head towards a large building—though not nearly as large as the tavern —surrounded by well-kempt gardens and a wrought iron fence. I frowned, trying to puzzle out why it looked familiar. I had never seen the building before, but its pointed spires and many stone carvings reminded me of something. When I figured out what it was, I staggered in shock.

"Is that a *church*?" I asked. Yolanda looked up at the building and back at me.

"Yes. Of course it is," she said. "What else would it be?"

"They have churches in Elsewhere? I just sort of thought that...I don't know, the supernatural had no purpose for God. Or gods or whatever. I mean with so much power at their finger tips, why bother worshipping something else?"

"The supernatural, as you say, probably understand more than others the limits of power," Yolanda scoffed. "Why, then, would they scorn someone who has so much? Not all are religious, true, but humans did not invent religion."

"You just rarely hear of things like werewolves and dragons in the same breath as, well God or gods," I said. Yolanda laughed at that and shook her head. We walked up the steps to the church and I looked at the building with wide-eyed curiosity. It looked exactly like a real church—Catholic or Anglican or something straight out of a gothic novel—except the carvings weren't of people or gargoyles. They were things like faeries and dragons and dwarves. I was about to go into the church when Yolanda caught my arm.

"It is commendable that you are curious, but the Order of the Silence is this way," she said, pulling me around the side of the edifice. We walked around the massive church and I saw where Yolanda was heading. A graveyard.

"Okay, hold on, I thought that the Order of Silence wasn't connected with Death. Just that Mercy worked for him on occasion," I said as we walked amongst the first tombstones. They were haphazardly arrayed, some straight and tall, others leaning with the words nearly faded to time. Even as we walked through the yard, I could feel something prowling around. It set my teeth on edge and made the hairs on the back of my neck stand on end. Yolanda stiffened and swallowed.

"They are not connected with Death. Directly. But the Order, ah, likes balance, and order from chaos," Yolanda said. Her voice was just a little too loud to be talking with me. The presence I sensed got closer. I started looking around as quickly as I could without getting whiplash, hoping that whatever was out there would make itself known. There was nothing quite as scary as something hunting you that you couldn't see.

"Yolanda," I said slowly, my voice wavering.

"Be still," the troll hissed through her teeth. She continued moving forwards, though, not helping at all. I did as I was told and froze. It's a good thing I did, too, because just as I stopped moving, something jumped through the spot I would have been had I taken another step.

The thing landed in a slide and slammed a slab-like shoulder against one of the tombstones, nearly shattering the stone. It turned and let out a low roar. I stared and tried not to look threatening. The thing was like a tiger and a lion had gotten together and birthed a rhinoceros-sized monster. It was definitely feline, its shoulders rippling with power. Its hindquarters were set on a lower line than its shoulders, like a hyena. The creature's neck was thick, holding up a head and muzzle that were bigger than most dogs. From its muzzle protruded two long fangs, thicker than two of my fingers. It had a slight stripe pattern to its pelt and no tail to speak of.

"Yolanda...when did sabre tooth cats become not extinct?" I squeaked. Yolanda was nowhere in sight. "Yolanda?"

The giant cat set its slitted eyes on me and let out a low, rumbling growl. It stepped forwards, its claws drawing gouges into the ground. The thing crouched, readying itself to leap at me. "Yolanda!" I said, trying not to edge into a scream.

The giant cat snarled, its fangs gleaming. From somewhere to my left, the troll bellowed, in reply to me or to the cat I wasn't sure, "We have an appointment!"

Immediately, the cat sat back on its haunches and regarded me in that haughty manner that the domestic versions had mastered. I staggered back and leaned against a tombstone to keep from falling over. I turned and saw Yolanda standing before a monument of some sort. There was a statue of a winged being with feathers sprouting off in different directions. It looked somewhat humanoid, but there was an eagle's beak and large, predatory eyes. At the base of its feet there was a stone cat, much like the one regarding me with quiet hunger. Only the stone one was much, much smaller.

"What *is* that?" I pointed at the feline.

"An Ennedi Tiger," a new voice said. I whipped around and saw a small, ancient man walking towards us. He wore deep green robes and had a staff that he leaned on for support. He had grey, wispy hair that stuck out in two tufts from the top of his head. His eyes were large and round and a deeper amber than Yolanda's. I don't know what it was, but there was something about him that made me think it would be really bad to cross him. Maybe it was the dispassionate look that he was giving me. Maybe it was the way the cat started purring. Or maybe it was the knicks and scratches in his staff.

"That's an Ennedi Tiger?" I asked, taking another look at the being. It regarded me cooly. I shivered. This was one of the things that had killed Magnus. For all I knew, it had been the one that actually killed Life's warrior. I might not have been able to die, but I doubted that I would enjoy living through having my guts opened up.

"A guardian. The protectors of balance. Much like the Order of Silence," the man said shuffling forwards. He came right up to me and I was a bit disconcerted to discover that he barely reached my hip. The tiny man appraised me with those enormous eyes and nodded firmly.

"We have an appointment," Yolanda repeated quieter. "We did not expect you to meet with us, Ancient One."

"When the matter is of such importance, then I feel obligated to involve myself," he said. Then he shuffled towards the monument, his staff looking like it was doing most of the work in propelling him forwards.

I looked at Yolanda in question. She mouthed "follow" to me. I did so, taking maybe one step for every three or four of the man's. The Ennedi Tiger watched me pass by with little more than quiet interest. I was fairly certain that if the Ancient One spoke, the Ennedi Tiger would happily disembowel me.

"Um, Ancient One," I said tentatively, "where are we going?"

"To the Order, of course," the tiny man said, blinking up at me. Then, he stepped through the monument and vanished. I made a sound in my throat and the Ennedi Tiger huffed.

"Seriously?" I demanded. Yolanda stuck out her chin belligerently.

"Follow him," she said. I shook my head. Being almost killed, injured, flying on a wyvern, meeting vampires, and everything else that had happened was all quite enough for me without requiring that I also walk through walls. Or statues. Whatever.

Yolanda seemed to disagree.

She stuck out one hand and gave me a very thorough shove. I yelped and fell through the statue. The world bent around me, colours becoming sounds and heat warming me from seemingly nowhere. I felt a little like my insides were being microwaved.

Then, I stumbled to my feet in the middle of an enormous stone cavern. There were stalactites falling from the ceiling and slick, dark stone wherever I looked. There were a few small lanterns hung from the walls. They gave off only enough light for you to sort of perceive the world. Details were blurred, shadows danced. And that prickling feeling I had felt in the graveyard? It had multiplied by about a thousand.

The Ancient One leaned on his staff and gave me a wide smile. I saw Mercy standing to one side, her head bowed in some sort of deference or respect, not making me feel any better at all.

"Welcome to the Order of Silence," the man said. "Would you like a tour?"

DEAD TO RIGHTS

I said a polite but firm no to a tour. Yolanda said yes. The troll pulled me aside to have a quiet word. I was fairly certain that the Ennedi Tiger, sitting in front of the place where we had come in and therefore blocking the exit, could hear everything we were saying. It made my stomach squirm.

"We don't have time for a tour," I whispered, all the while keeping a jovial smile on my face. Just in case the Ancient One was watching closely.

"We cannot disrespect our hosts," Yolanda argued, also looking pleasantly serene.

"You were the one who said that we can't allow the imbalance to continue any longer," I pointed out, nodding seriously. Yolanda allowed herself a small head-shake of disbelief before she smiled.

"The purpose of the Order of Silence is the balance," Yolanda said. "It would do no harm to allow a tour. You might even learn something without having to step on anyone's toes to do it."

"Hey!" I protested. "I haven't stepped on anyone's toes yet. I have been attacked and kidnapped and murdered more than once. But I haven't stepped on anyone's toes."

"I wasn't being literal," Yolanda sighed. I frowned.

"Neither was I."

Yolanda just stared at me, waiting. Almost pouting. I was the one who was meant to be in charge, here. She was my assistant. This was my investigation. But by George, Yolanda had me doing exactly what she wanted. I chalked it up to her knowing more about Elsewhere than I did. But after this whole debacle, we were going to have a serious talk about who was actually the boss.

I turned to the Ancient One, a smile plastered on my face. "We'd love a tour!"

"Good," the small man nodded, making his tufts of hair bounce a little. He would have been a comical character if he weren't so...I don't know what it was, but something told me not to mess with him. Especially not with a giant feline killing machine sitting not too far away. Or with Mercy by his side.

The tour started off with the main cavern—the entrance to the Order, which was reached by a symbolic representation of the balance that the Order loved so much. That is, it was connected symbolically to the place where Life and Death met, where the balance began, my host informed us with a fond smile.

Apparently, that place was a graveyard. Any graveyard. Provided you knew how to contact the Order, that was the place you went. That bizarre and not terribly helpful explanation done, we went to the side caverns.

"This is where we train our initiates in the art of balance," the Ancient One said, sweeping a hand out to indicate the room. It was little more than a poorly lit bare cavern with a smooth floor, with a collection of people there. They were doing some sort of Tai Chi, except it wasn't an individual sport. They were paired off, doing the slow motions against the other person, bringing their hands up to block or sweep or whatever the term was. As I watched, they slowly sped up, each hit coming faster and faster until it was nothing more than a blur.

One of the pairs closest to us was going faster than the others. They looked like Mercy and Justice in their inhuman looks and their wind-like motions, only younger and less powerful: aurai. I was about to say something along the lines of, "Wow," when one of the aurai hit the other directly in the chest. The aurai flew backwards, slamming into the wall.

The room stopped moving. Every one of the people in pairs froze in whatever position they were in. Only their eyes tracked to their fallen compatriot. The aurai who had hit the wall managed a groan and tried to stand. Mercy barked out a harsh word that I couldn't understand and the aurai stopped moving. The Ancient One tottered forwards and poked at the aurai with his staff.

"Hmm...This one has not yet grasped the principles of balance," he said, half to himself. "He will need reconditioning."

Two of the frozen people—more aurai, though they could have been elves—moved at his words and hauled the fallen one to his feet. They dragged him out of the room, the injured aurai letting out cries of protest. Silence reigned. Slowly, the others began to go through their movements again, starting at a snail's pace and slowly growing faster. No one looked to the place where the fallen aurai had been taken.

"What was that about?" I asked as we moved on. "And is everyone here an aurai?"

"Not everyone," Mercy said. "But many. It is a great honour for those of the air to be trained in keeping the balance. Life or death, the air does not care. It only keeps doing its job. For us, it is balance."

"Uh-huh. So what's this 'reconditioning' thing?"

"The initiate will be brought to understand the balance. To stand on the ledge between life and death and know what it means for balance to reign." The Ancient One smiled serenely, leaning on his staff and blinking up at me with those wide eyes.

"To stand on the ledge between life and death," I muttered to Yolanda, trying to maintain a pleasant expression. "What does that mean?"

Yolanda swallowed audibly, the sound echoing off the cavern walls. She blanched at the sound, turning a light greyish-green, and watched Mercy and the tiny man for any sign that they had heard. Then, she leaned over and breathed in my ear, "Torture. Until almost the point of death. And then brought back. Again and again and again."

I stopped moving, completely flabbergasted. How could this be possible? Scratch that. I knew *how* it could be possible, I just didn't believe that anyone was crazy enough to want to do such a thing. It was cruel and beyond idiotic. To torture someone until they understood *balance*?

I understood why and how Mercy could be an assassin.

Bile rose in my throat, but I forced myself to swallow it down. There was nothing I could do that these people would listen to or understand. I didn't have the resources to stop it. It might have been wrong, but I couldn't do anything about it. Not without ruining any chance of fixing the balance that these people revered so much. And right now, with the task that I had been set, that was pretty much a bad idea.

For the rest of the tour, I couldn't help but see blood splattered in the shadows of the lights that flickered over the cavern walls. The people who passed us weren't superstitious protectors of balance, they were zealots. And they smiled at me.

The Ancient One jabbered away, describing scenes carved out of the stone in order to dedicate a life to the balance of art and immutability. There were caverns for every religion known to mortal and immortal kind. Christianity, Hinduism, Taoism, Judaism, Islam, Buddhism, Paganism, more. I couldn't help but feel a twinge of sadness as we passed these places that were meant to be sacred.

I shook my head and stuffed my hands into my pockets, focusing on putting one foot in front of the other. I tuned out the descriptions that the Ancient One was giving. These people who killed to protect the balance. Who tortured. Caused pain. Somehow, I doubt that causing suffering helped.

Unfortunately, I also needed them, this Order of Silence. They had control of the Ennedi Tigers. So I walked along like a docile marketing agent. I let Yolanda do the talking, though, just in case I said something irreversibly stupid.

Finally, we found ourselves in a small cavern that was decorated—disturbingly—much like my office. The desk was old and heavy wood, the chairs were modern and comfortable. The back walls had been carved out into bookshelves. There was no computer, but it was familiar enough to send shivers up my spine.

"So," the old man asked, sitting in his chair with an exhalation of relief. Yolanda and I sank carefully into the chairs opposite his desk. Mercy strode behind the desk to stand behind the Ancient One like some sort of sentinel. "Why did you call for an appointment?"

I looked at Yolanda, who kept her mouth firmly closed. Now she was acting as my assistant, was she? Figures. Still, there was nothing else to do, so I spoke. My anger at the cruel idiocy of the Order might have coloured my words; they came out as more of a direct accusation than a question.

"We learned that someone used an Ennedi Tiger in order to kill a human. One of Life's warriors or champions or whatever," I said. "This person also decided to circumvent Death in the matter."

The old man's staff clattered to the floor. Mercy's every muscle tensed and she reached for the belt at her hip, where a knife was sheathed. I just sat there, pushed my glasses up my nose and let my lip curl ever so slightly.

"The balance has been skewed?!" the Ancient One wheezed, holding a hand to his chest.

"Indeed," I monotoned.

"This is terrible! For Death to gain power over Life, for the balance to have shifted...this could bring about the end of the world!" The Ancient One was almost shouting by the end of this statement. Mercy patted his shoulders gently. There was enough emotion in her normally emotionless face to tell me that she was shocked by the news as much as the Ancient One. That, or she was concerned for his reaction.

"Death sent me and my assistant to fix this," I said. I crossed an ankle over my knee and gave a *hmmm*. "Actually, in point of fact, Death sent me to find whoever has done this so *he* can fix it."

Mercy paled, her earthy skin looking sickly against her white hair. She may have had a smooth countenance, but there were some things you couldn't hide. "You think that someone at the Order has done this?"

"Why not?" I asked, shrugging. "You are, after all, the only ones that use Ennedi Tigers, aren't you?"

"Our tigers are trained to guard the balance!" the Ancient One insisted. "They would never be used in such a manner. They wouldn't go against their training."

"Really? Then tell me who else trains these sabres and I'll be on my merry way," I said. The Ancient One and Mercy exchanged a glance. "I thought not. So, who has the influence to get an Ennedi Tiger to go against its training?"

And, for that matter, who amongst these zealots would want to upset the balance?

"No," the Ancient One said, pounding his fist against the desk. "No one in the Order would dare go against the balance."

"Unless they were a traitor," I pointed out. "Come, now, surely you can't say that everyone is absolutely devoted to the balance? I mean, you *torture* people to break them into obedience."

"We condition their minds to understand what balance means," Mercy said, her tone cold.

"Torture is torture," I replied, just as coldly. "These people aren't giving their devotion of their own free will. They're being broken into it. As far as I'm concerned, that just leaves a whole lot of people who have the means and motive to upset the balance."

"You don't understand our ways, human. Every single one of those who comes to us knows what awaits them. They choose this life because to serve and protect the balance is supreme," the tiny Ancient One said. He reached out his hand and his fallen staff flew upwards into it. Magic. Oh, dear. I swallowed, my anger abating in favour of nervousness.

"Do you think those who walk casually through their lives ever achieve the perfect balance we strive to protect? That they can understand what is at *stake* when the balance is upset? Or wouldn't they much prefer to have Life triumph over Death? Those of us here, we understand. We understand how terrible it would be if no one were to ever die. We understand how the world would fall apart if life were so fragile. Those foolish people wouldn't be able to live so freely, so ignorantly, if they didn't have us to protect them."

I may not have understood the whole point of the Order—I certainly didn't understand volunteering for torture—but I did understand one thing: that was disgust colouring the Ancient One's tone. He actively hated those who weren't of the Order. Which meant Yolanda. Which meant me. And I had just insinuated that there was a traitor among them.

I held out my hands in a peace offering. "Look, I get that the balance between Life and Death is important. But can you honestly say that people don't understand?" I shook my head. "No, it doesn't matter. That's not why I'm here."

"You are not here to question the Order? To accuse one of us of failing our most basic duty?" the Ancient One sneered. I looked at Mercy for help, hoping that she would intervene on my behalf. Or Yolanda. But my assistant and the assassin were both silent. This was my accusation and my argument to make.

Goody.

"I'm here to find out who killed by circumventing Death," I said. "That's all. Look, whoever did this upset the balance in favour of Death, right?" I looked at Yolanda in pure desperation.

She finally piped up, now that I wasn't about to offend anyone. "If Death holds more power than Life, many will die. Immortals who should have centuries more to live. Mortals, whose lives are already short will end early. There will be many who will never get a chance to live."

"Thus upsetting the balance further, yes, we know," the Ancient One growled.

"Well, who would want such a thing?" I asked.

"Besides Death?" the Ancient One said, very pointedly I might add.

"Yes," I sighed, "*besides* Death."

"I do not know," the Ancient One replied.

This could not be going any worse.

"Okay, think," I said, partly to myself, mostly to Yolanda and the two balance-fanatics. "If Death got the control, then who would benefit? Murderers, maybe? Predators?"

"Each predator is another predator's prey," Mercy said, calm logic in the face of my more-desperate variety. Oddly enough, I got the impression that she was trying to help. She had been there when Life accused Death, when the situation was revealed, and she hadn't told the Ancient One anything about it. I had been the one to do that. Which either made her very suspicious or not nearly as fanatical as I thought. Or, perhaps, she was just being merciful. But to whom?

"So we rule out basic predators," I said. "Fine. Who does that leave? Demons? Beings that thrive on death?"

"They only have power in the mortal world," Yolanda said. "They were bound aeons ago."

"Still, there would be lots of people dying. A whole global reset. The apocalypse. End of the world as we know it, time to start over—" I sat up straight, every muscle in my body singing. "A reset. Starting over."

"The balance would not change how the world works, not unless it is further circumvented," the Ancient One said.

"Not right away," I shook my head. "But over time, those who survived would get a chance to start over. All of the horrors and corruption and lies of the old world. Poof, gone. So many miserable people put, well, out of their misery. People who didn't value Life. Who didn't fight for Life. Who didn't care about Death. Pretty much every person I've ever met."

"Cal," Yolanda said, a warning tone in her voice. "Be careful."

"Who would want that? Hmm?" I looked up at the woman standing perfectly still at the side of her leader. "It would be a mercy to end their pointless, *ignorant*, lives. Wouldn't it?"

Mercy shivered, though from the way her breath hitched, I doubted it was from cold. "It would," she said. "But I did not do it."

I sat back in my chair, ready to challenge her, when

the Ancient One slammed the end of his staff into the floor. "You dare to come here and accuse the most devoted of our order of something like this?" he snarled, eyes literally blazing. With fire and everything.

"I—"

"You have accused the Order of standing against the balance. You have committed a crime against us. It is just as well that you came here of your own free will," the tiny, now-flaming, man hissed.

"Now wait just a—"

"You will be reconditioned." He slammed the staff on the stones once more. "Take him away!"

DEAD WRONG

"This is a mistake," I said. My captors—not aurai, but bigger and tougher warrior types with claws and fangs that didn't fit into their maws— were dragging me by my arms. We were moving fast enough that I couldn't get my feet underneath me. As a result, I had very little chance to either walk in a dignified manner or, more importantly, fight to run away.

"There is no mistake," the big woman on my left said. She had eyes slitted like a cat and hissed a little when she spoke.

"No, actually, I'm pretty sure there is," I said. "I haven't done anything!"

"You accused the Order of working against the balance," the man on my right snapped. "And you all but charged Grand Master Mercy of starting the apocalypse."

Grand Master Mercy? What was this, the Illuminati?

"Look, no. I was just thinking out loud. I believe Mercy when she said she didn't do it! What about the sanctity of an appointment? What about the fact that I don't belong to your Order?!" I yelped, my toes catching on a particularly sharp piece of cave rock. The funny thing was, I actually did believe Mercy. There had been too much shock and horror in her normally-expressionless face to be anything but genuine.

My guards didn't care. They were going to do whatever they were told to do and that meant they were taking me to be tortured. I had to find another way out of my current predicament. I looked around, hoping to see Yolanda pounding up behind me with some of her troll battle magic, but she was nowhere to be seen. Actually, she hadn't protested as much as I thought she would have. Sure, she protested and yelled and stamped her feet a bit, but when it came down to it, Yolanda hadn't tried to fight my guards.

I had. Vehemently.

Maybe she was going to go find Death and get him to sort this out. After all, she may have been a troll and possessed of battle-magic, but she was only one person. The Order of Silence were a bunch of trained assassins.

I lost track of the caverns we had passed while I was being dragged off. Granted, I was pretty much geographically challenged to begin with, but I couldn't manage more than "two lefts and a right" at the beginning of the trip before things went wonky and confused. When the guards dragged me into a cave that was darker and more oppressive than the rest, I therefore had no idea where I was and no idea how to get out, even if I could manage to finagle an escape.

This cave was clear of stalactites, but stalagmites rose from the ground in varying degrees of thickness and pointiness. One of the more knife-like ones had an initiate impaled on it by his shoulder, bent backwards so all his weight was resting on the injury. He was paler than Justice, but with Mercy's white hair. He tried to stand at an angle so the pressure on his back would be less, and keep the stalagmite from sinking deeper into him. I recognised the aurai from earlier, though the rest of him was scratched up and bloody. I choked back what little lunch I had eaten and blinked away my dizziness.

The initiate didn't look anything like a willing supporter of the Order. He was crying and muttering pleas under his breath. He fixed his eyes on me and I saw a faint flicker of hope fill them. "Help me," he mouthed. I struggled more against my guards, but they held me fast. The hope in the aurai's eyes died and I felt it draining from me, too.

At least the aurai had the ability to die.

I was thrown into a corner, hitting my shoulder hard enough for something to crack and pop. I snarled in pain and ended up sounding a lot more defiant than I had expected. The female warrior leaned over and sneered, showing her teeth. I could see she had a forked, snake-like tongue. I didn't know what she was, but I had a feeling she was a lot more dangerous than I was.

"You will soon be dancing to our tune, *human*. Fighting will do you no good," she hissed. I wanted to muster the will to do something heroically stupid, like spitting in her face or swinging at her with a right hook. All I managed was a moan of pain.

The male warrior chained my hands to the wall behind me. Heavy manacles weighed down my wrists and bit into my hands as I moved. The guards took a moment to laugh in my face, then sauntered off to who knows where. I slumped against the wall, muscles shaking. I didn't have much strength left in me, and certainly not to fight where it was useless.

"You are not an initiate."

I jumped and got my arms wrenched for my effort. I looked around wildly, but the only people in the cavern were me and the aurai impaled on the rock. Which meant... "You can still *talk*?!"

"They would not cut out my tongue," the aurai panted. His voice was twisted and in obvious pain, but he was coherent and clear. I was astonished and weirdly impressed. "I may have need of it later in my life with the Order."

"Sure, because they want assassins that will talk you to death," I scoffed. I shifted, the manacles clinking against the chain. "Look, I don't mean to pry, but do you really believe that this, this 'torture to achieve balance' is a good thing?"

The initiate let out a sound somewhere between a laugh and a groan of pain. As I watched, he accidentally shifted so that the rock twisted in his shoulder. The aurai's face grew pale and he took a couple of shaky breaths. He licked his lips and spoke, "I was not informed of such things when I joined the Order."

"It seems like that would be something you should know," I said. "I only came for an appointment and look at me. I would think they tell initiates these things. Especially since the Ancient One and her Grandmasterness Mercy seem to think that everyone volunteers for this."

"Those who join the Order believe in protecting the balance," the aurai panted. Sweat was starting to plaster his hair to his head, making the white locks appear silver. "I believed in the honour of my bloodline. My uncle joined the Order, and his father before him, and so on back for centuries."

"Why don't you leave, then?" I asked.

"Once they have 'conditioned' you, they believe they own you," the aurai said, voice pained. He took a breath that sent shudders through this body. "The only way to pass the conditioning is to swear an oath to protect the balance with every ounce of your life and until your death."

"These guys are absolutely insane," I concluded. That didn't exactly bode well to me. I looked around at the various instruments of torture in the cave. Most of them weren't more than pointy pieces of metal, but some looked as though they had very specific functions. Given that I couldn't die, I was either about to go through a very serious amount of pain or give in to whatever they wanted. Whatever *that* was.

"Look," I said, pulling myself together enough to look at the sylph without shaking apart. "I'm going to get out of here. And when I do, I'm going to take you with me."

"They will not allow it," the aurai said. "I must endure this until they deem me worthy again. Either that or I will die, and serve the balance that way."

"How about you don't," I said. "One way or another, we're getting out of here. They may not have been responsible for killing Magnus, but these people need to be taken apart. So I'm going to make it my grand mission in life. And I'll need your help."

"How can you be so sure of this?" the aurai asked.

"Oh, you know, because it's the only option I've got. Well, the only real option," I said. "Besides, I work with some very determined people. And my job's not done yet. I can't believe that I'm going to be down here forever, being tortured by a cult of insane people."

"You wouldn't be down here forever," the aurai rasped. He licked his lips again and I wondered how long he had been without water. Even if it had been only an hour or so since he'd been dragged away before my very eyes, it was too long. "Only until you die and serve the balance that way."

"Like I said. Forever."

The aurai looked at me in confusion. Just at that moment, a new person walked into the room. When I say walked, I really mean slithered. This person had a human torso and snake trunk, complete with rattle on the end. His— hers—its skin was the same poisonous green as the scales of the snake parts and I could see fangs dripping a dangerous bluish liquid. It hissed when it hit the ground. Note to self: stay away from poisonous fangs.

"Human," the snake-person hissed. "It has been an age since I have had a human life to play with. So fragile, but so evocative. You feel things so much *deeper* than most immortals."

"That's great, but I'm actually not all that keen on being tortured," I said. "I work for Death and he's going to be mightily displeased when he learns of this."

"Who you work for is of no interest to me," the snake snapped. It grabbed a small knife like a scalpel. It was just about then that I realised something very important. I was absolutely terrified of pain. The last couple of days had given me enough insight to know this for sure.

"That's unfortunate," I said, my voice two notes higher than usual. "Because when I signed on with Death, he disconnected me from my life-force."

"What does tha —"

"I can't die," I squeaked. "I can't die. I'm not living and so I can't die. No matter what you do to me, I won't swear to join your idiotic cult. And you can't kill me, so the balance is never going to be served with me."

The snake hissed, rattling its tail. "We shall see about that."

It lunged for me and swiped the scalpel across my throat. For the second time in as many days, someone slit my throat with the intent to kill. And, annoyingly, for the second time in as many days, it failed to kill me.

I coughed my way back to consciousness mere moments after the snake had attempted to kill me. "Seriously?! That was your solution?"

The snake backed away from me—an odd thing to see in a reptile. It said something in a foreign language that was mostly hisses and buzzing. Then, the snake dropped the knife, turned tail and fled.

"Well, now what?" I asked the aurai. Despite being in obvious pain, he just threw back his head and started laughing. He pushed against the stone and let out a gasp of pain, but a smile still lit his features.

"Now, we may actually have a hope of getting out of here," he panted, teeth flashing in the dim light.

"In case you haven't noticed, I'm still chained to a wall and you're, well, you've been stabbed in the shoulder by a rock." I jingled my chains to prove my point. The aurai shook his head and pushed himself against the rock again. I realised that he wasn't just struggling, he was making an active effort to lift himself off the rock. With his back bowed backwards, he couldn't get enough leverage to really do anything, but he was trying.

"Don't you see? You cannot be killed. You are not attached to a life-force in the way that even us immortals are," the aurai said. He screwed up his features and pushed with everything he had. It was still not enough. There were several inches of stone protruding from his shoulder and all he was doing was tearing the wound larger.

"Stop!" I cried, pulling against the manacles. I couldn't do anything to help him.

"Ngggh," the aurai grunted. "No. I c-can do this!"

"You're going to do more damage," I insisted.

"We will get free and the Order can't do anything about it," the aurai growled. He shuffled his feet so that his back was bowed backwards even more, then pushed himself upwards. He gained another two inches before he couldn't move anymore.

"As far as I can see, we're trapped here," I said, hoping my words wouldn't provoke this guy into doing anything even more stupid.

"You really are as ignorant as you appear," the aurai chuckled. I was pretty certain the pain had gone to his head. "You are not connected to a life-force. You cannot die."

"Yes, we've established this fact. Which is why the snake-thing tried to slit my throat," I said. "And why I'm now standing in a puddle of my own blood, with no apparent wound."

"But this means that you are neither alive nor dead," the aurai said. "The Order has no power over you. You are not within their system of balance, because you cannot be alive, nor can you be killed. It's why they fight for the balance in the first place. Because Death and Life are too powerful for them to control. If those two got it in their head to change things, the Order could do nothing. So they try to keep the world around

Life and Death in balance, in the hopes that it will maintain peace. You're not a part of their battle!"

"As much as I love not being part of their battle," I said, "we still have one problem. We're trapped down here. And I may not be able to die, but I can still be tortured. I feel plenty of pain."

"The Order wouldn't dare. You are as close to the balance as they're ever going to get. You walk the line between Life and Death." The aurai let out a bark of laughter, then groaned in pain. I was afraid he was going to pass out, but apparently everybody in the entire world of the Elsewhere is tougher than I am.

"So, what, I'm some sort of ideal?" I said. "A sacred relic?"

"We would not put it like that."

I jumped as far as the manacles would allow. The Ancient One was standing in the entrance to the cave, leaning on his staff and wearing a very displeased expression. Mercy stood just behind him, her face as expressionless as ever. I still got the distinct impression she wasn't pleased. Maybe it was the way she had her hands clenched into fists. Behind them was Yolanda, looking rather the more worse for wear. She had a cut over one eye and a swollen lip. Her knuckles were bleeding, too. But she was whole and grinning at me with no small amount of pleasure.

She hadn't abandoned me after all, even against such impossible odds.

The snake-person who was going to torture me was

behind Yolanda, looking extremely uncertain. Its eyes kept flickering to me and it rang its hands nervously.

"We do not know what you are, but you are correct," the Ancient One said, curling his lip. "We have no providence over you. There is nothing we can do to you, nor should we. You walk the balance."

Mercy stepped forwards, holding a set of keys in her hands. She strode towards me and knelt to undo the manacles around my wrists. "How?" she asked with a breath. I could hear the longing in her voice. "How did you come to be part of the balance?"

I shrugged, rubbing my raw wrists gently. "Death offered me a job. I took it."

"But...you are no more than human," Mercy said in almost a plea. "Please, tell me."

"I have told you, Mercy," I lay a hand on her shoulder. I didn't like her, I didn't like what she believed, I was terrified of her occupation, but that didn't mean I wanted her to suffer. I just couldn't give her what she wanted. "There is nothing more."

She slumped her shoulders barely half-an-inch, but it was enough to tell me that this had been a real blow. I doubted very much we would ever be friends. Actually, I had probably made an enemy. Given the look on the Ancient One's face, I had probably made more than one. I walked over to the aurai initiate, who had watched everything in silence, trying to catch his breath through the pain.

"Do you want to be here?" I asked him, loudly

enough that there could be no doubt of the Ancient One's hearing.

"No," he breathed. I nodded and looked at Yolanda. She walked over and helped me lift the injured creature off the stalagmite. He cried out in pain as we freed him. Then, he finally relaxed, his legs trembling. Yolanda let him lean on her.

"Right then," I said, glaring at the Ancient One. "We're going. You've made it perfectly clear that you had nothing to do with the death of Magnus, Ennedi Tiger or no."

"Indeed," the Ancient One sneered. "We wish you well on your journey of balance, human."

"It's Cal. My name is Cal. Really, it's not that hard," I said. "One whole syllable less than 'human.'"

"Escort them out," the Ancient One hissed to Mercy. She bowed her head and led us out. I didn't pay any more attention to the caves the second time around. I doubted I would ever be invited back here, and I didn't care to memorise this place. I ignored the stares of the initiates and full members of the Order. Yolanda didn't pay them any attention, either. She just walked straight on after Mercy, letting the exhausted and injured aurai lean on her.

We emerged in the graveyard where we had gone in without even the Ennedi tiger as escort. Mercy didn't say goodbye, just turned back around and vanished into the monument. I took a moment to rest, sitting on the top of a headstone.

"I haven't been here a full week and I've already

offended a cult, ticked off an all-knowing Irishman, and killed a vampire. Oh, and I haven't finished my first task for Death," I said. I looked at the aurai, still leaning against Yolanda. He stared at me in wide-eyed astonishment. "I'm Cal Thorpe," I said. "I'm Death's marketing agent."

"Agravaine," the aurai said breathlessly. "It is good to meet you, Cal."

"You, too."

He took the opportunity to succumb to gravity and pass out.

I sat on that stone for a good while longer before I spoke. While I waited, I rubbed the raw skin on my wrists, as though the pain would wake me up. It didn't, but I kept rubbing at my skin. Finally, I took a breath and looked up at Yolanda. "We've gotten nowhere. That lead with the Ennedi Tiger was all we had. Fionn thought it dangerous enough that he had to kill me for it, and it led nowhere."

Yolanda nodded. "I thought the Order would have known something."

"All we got from them was a good deal of outrage and an almost-torture session. Mercy didn't do it," I said. "And no one else there would be stupid enough to upset their precious 'balance' by doing it."

"Then there must have been another reason for killing Magnus that we don't know about," Yolanda reasoned. I nodded.

"I feared as much. My only problem is that we've run out of people in Elsewhere who knew something,"

I said. "Unless you can think of another force that might have had access to an Ennedi Tiger and might have wanted to kill Life's favourite person."

Yolanda shook her head.

"Well, then we're going to have to figure out how in the world to find out more about Magnus."

"We will have to go to the mortal realms," Yolanda said. She didn't sound terribly thrilled about the prospect. At this point, I couldn't blame her. Everywhere this miserable investigation had led us was full of pain and violence and a whole lot of things that really wanted to kill me. I didn't think that investigating the life and times of a successful jewel thief on Earth was really going to be much better.

Maybe if Magnus were nothing more than a fisherman. Or a banker. Or anything other than a jewel thief. I had a feeling things were going to be just as complicated and dangerous.

"A couple of problems," I said. "Death said I couldn't return to the mortal realms. He said something about having removed me from the timeline or fate or whatever. And you're...you're a troll. How are you going to blend in?"

Yolanda grinned at me. "Humans are very stupid," she said. "They don't know a troll from a rock. Ah, no offence."

"None taken," I muttered. I sighed. "Alright, let's get Agravaine the aurai to Doc Graveltoes. Then I have to see a guy about a travel pass."

"Can we get popcorn when we're there?"

WAITING FOR DEATH

*A*gravaine was dutifully delivered to Graveltoes, who clucked over the aurai's wounds and shooed Yolanda and me out of the hospital. I think he was growing just as tired of me as I was of him, but according to Yolanda, he was the best to help Agravaine. When we got to the annoyingly familiar street, I looked around for any other vampires or people trying to kill or kidnap me. Given my recent experiences, I felt just fine being slightly paranoid. To my relief, though, there were no vampires, no members of the Order waiting with ritualistic swords or torture devices, not even a slightly furious wyvern. However, Iggy and the Rolls Royce were waiting for us. I looked at Yolanda in question.

"I thought we weren't going to be availing ourselves of Iggy's services," I said slowly. "That he worked for Death and wasn't going to ferry us from place to place."

The chauffeur looked at me with those pinprick fires that he had for eyes and raised his eyebrows.

"Iggy?" he rumbled. "Hmmph."

The door to the back of the Rolls opened and Death's voice greeted me, "I am not certain Yggdral appreciates the nickname, Cal."

Yolanda shrugged sheepishly. "I called him while you were arguing—er, talking—with Graveltoes."

I sighed through my nose and just climbed into the car. Death waved his hand and the Rolls expanded enough so that there were two seats facing each other, like a modern limousine. Even with Yolanda in the car, we all fit comfortably. If I weren't so freaked out by that particular magic, I would have been very impressed. Death reached into a small console and pulled out a cut-glass decanter with a deep liquid inside.

"Cognac?" he asked casually.

"No, thanks," I said. Yolanda shook her head. "Did Yolanda fill you in on everything?"

Death poured himself a drink. He swirled it slowly in the glass and sipped. There was a pause while he let the cognac settle on his tongue. Then, "She did. Apparently you have developed a side-effect that I had not anticipated."

"That's not really the most important issue right—wait, you didn't mean for this to happen? For me to not be able to die?" I gaped. My glasses slipped down my nose.

"Indeed not," Death replied, though he sounded

more interested than frustrated. "I had meant for you to simply become an immortal, much like many that inhabit Elsewhere. I thought separating you from your life-force was the best way to go about that. My touch does that, amongst other things, but I had not also realised the implications when I did not kill you afterwards."

I shook my head. "Hold on. So your touch separates a person from their life-force. And then you kill them. But because you didn't kill me, no one else can kill me either? I thought you had done this before."

"Did I give you that impression? Oh, dear, I am sorry," Death said, hiding his smile behind his glass. "I am an extraordinarily powerful being. I do not often go about displaying that power for the purpose of experimentation. The consequences would be too dire. It is quite interesting, though."

"Great," I said hoarsely. "So what am I supposed to do, now?"

"As you were doing," Death said easily. "Yolanda informed me that you have not proceeded terribly far with your investigation here in Elsewhere. 'Dead ends' was the phrase she used."

"Yeah, we eliminated the only people who had easy access to the murder weapon. An Ennedi Tiger," I said, ignoring Death's pun.

"Indeed. A very provocative weapon, and not one easily used. I have never heard of anyone besides the Order of Silence using the tigers in any official capacity, though they used to cause havoc in Africa before they were tamed. Are you quite certain that it was not the Order who perpetrated this, ah, crime?" Death swirled the drink in his glass, and I swore I saw a glimpse of the caves where I had been killed—again—flash there. I blinked and swallowed.

"The Ancient One seemed apoplectic at the thought. And the only one—unless all the people they tortured into compliance decided to rebel—with a motive, was Mercy. But I don't think she did it."

Yolanda shook her head. "Mercy would not do such a thing."

"I think you underestimate her, my dear troll," Death murmured. He inclined his head. "However, I am inclined to agree with you. Mercy may be...capable, but she would be unlikely to act of her own free will. She is too devoted to the Order. And your idea of a rebellion, Cal, while amusing, is unlikely. Had you not freed your new aurai friend when you did, he would be as thoroughly loyal as the rest of them."

I frowned, glancing out the window towards the hospital. I didn't like the idea that torture could be so effective. As far as I was concerned, it was beyond wrong. And weren't there studies and such that said it wasn't terribly useful as an interrogation tool? Then, that had been in the mortal realms, with mortal people. Immortals, on the other hand, were something entirely different.

"The use of the Ennedi tiger is very interesting," Death continued, though he sounded nothing more than mildly bored, "but I fear it will not lead you anywhere. Certainly not soon enough to avoid an altercation between my wife and myself. What other lines of inquiry had you thought to pursue?"

I shifted in the seat, thinking that maybe that drink sounded good right about then. "Now we need to know more about Magnus. It just doesn't make sense that he would be completely unconnected to Elsewhere. How else would someone know about him? I mean, Life doesn't seem to go about advertising her relationship with her champions, because she doesn't want you to take them from her. So someone else had to find out about him. Right?"

Death took a deep breath. He let it out with a smile. "Life is indeed afraid that I will take her champions from her, as I always do. Such is the nature of our relationship. All that lives will die. So she savours every moment—in private, as you assume. Yes, then, you would be correct. Magnus must have had some connection to Elsewhere, or he would likely still be alive now."

I was the one to take a breath, this time. I hoped this worked, and that Death would let me get on with my investigation the way that I needed. If not, well, then this whole thing would be over. "I don't think that we're going to learn of Magnus' connection to Elsewhere from, well, Elsewhere."

"You need to venture to the mortal realms." Death nodded sagely. "Very well."

My mouth dropped open. "I thought you said I couldn't go back!"

"I said you could not return to your previous life," Death said. "Travel to the mortal realms is relatively easy. I need only provide you with an alternate identity. Though, I do warn you, even if you were to encounter someone you knew, Cal, they would not know you. Their mind could suffer damage trying to fill in the gaps on who you are and why they feel they know you. Those who were closest to you would suffer the worst."

"Gotcha," I grumbled. "Brain damage if I try to talk to anyone I knew. Well, we're going to Norway, so that shouldn't be too much of an issue."

The thought of returning to the mortal realms, even if it was very far away from everything and anyone I had ever known, set my heart pounding. I could feel my palms start to sweat and rubbed them on my knees. There was no need to get excited, I told myself. It was hardly going to be as awe-inspiring as Elsewhere. There would be no wyverns, no mansions and palaces, no fancy new social media that was both amazing and made no sense. It wouldn't even be home.

But it would be close enough.

Death appraised me for a moment, then he nodded once. "Very well," he said again. He waved his hand and two amulets appeared there. They were little more than silver circles, but when I took mine, I could feel it pulsing with power.

"These will provide you with the appropriate identities in the mortal realms," Death said. "Should someone ask you questions, you need only say what the amulets prompt you to say. You will have all the necessary documentation as you require. Be warned, they only work on mortals. Were you to run into anything from Elsewhere, it could be quite problematic."

"We'll be careful, Master," Yolanda said eagerly.

I just nodded and slipped my amulet over my neck. It was like stepping into a pool, except I stayed perfectly dry. When I moved my hands, it felt like I was pushing against water. It wasn't hard, it just took more effort than usual. "That's weird," I said, waving my hand about.

"The amulets were designed to work in the mortal realms," Death said, smiling slightly. "They will feel as such until you arrive."

"If I look into a mirror, will I see myself or someone else?" I asked, staring at my hand. If I looked hard enough, I could see the light bending around the appendage.

"Why don't you go find out?" Death asked. He clapped his hands together. He vanished, along with Iggy, the car, and everything else.

DEATH AND TAXES

Travelling through worlds this time was nothing like walking through the monument or travelling with Thaddeus as a shadow. One moment, I was sitting in the car with Yolanda and Death, the next, I was suspended four feet above a knoll that was more rock than grass. I flailed my arms and fell. I couldn't do anything to get my feet under me and landed very hard on my bum.

"Ow," I said.

Yolanda landed a lot harder than I did, but she didn't seem to be hurt, either. Rock trolls, as has been previously established, are a lot tougher than humans. "Death always makes the smoothest transitions," Yolanda said. She stood and brushed herself off. "Once, I took a Fae portal. I was sick for days."

"Good to know," I mumbled, crawling to my feet. I looked around.

"Where are we?" Yolanda asked, peering around

with one hand up to shield her eyes from the sun. I copied her and took survey of the land.

"I'd say we're about a hundred feet from the cabin where Magnus died." I pointed to the stone-and-wood structure. "I didn't see the outside, when Life showed me her memory, but I saw enough. Besides, there's yellow tape."

"Yellow tape means something to you?" Yolanda asked, following behind me as I walked up to the cabin.

"Yellow tape, so I have been told, means a crime scene." I peered through the windows and saw the same rustic setting from Life's memory. Including a large blood-stain on the floor. "This is definitely it."

"And what would you being doing here at a crime scene?"

The new voice made me jump. It was sort of garbled, like someone had put an overlay on the words to make them sound like English. The person it belonged to was of average height, average looks, good working clothes. Best of all, he was human. Completely, normally, perfectly human. He was also a cop. I gathered that much from the fact that his badge was glinting in the sunlight from a chain around his neck.

"Ah, yes," I said. My words also came out garbled and I frowned. Yolanda looked at me, and for a moment, I saw another image of her superimposed on the one of the troll I knew. She was tall, for a human woman, built heavily and definitely not on the attractive end of the scale. But the image was also human. The amulets, I realised. They were making us blend in. Probably even translating to and from Norwegian.

I was going to have fun with this.

"We are here to discover what, exactly, happened to the man who died here," I said, putting a bite of aggression in my tone. I reached into my pockets and, sure enough, a pad and pen were readily available just as I had imagined they would be. "I heard that it was a wild animal, but from the way you lot whisked the body away and have kept an active guard here, I'd say that whatever happened was a whole lot more than a wild animal. Or was the victim just that important?"

The cop said a word that the amulet didn't translate into English, looking like he had swallowed a mouthful of vinegar. "Reporters," he growled. I shrugged and held my pen to the paper.

"Anything to say, ah, Officer....?" I prompted.

"Janos," he said, less than agreeably. "Detective Janos."

"A detective! Well, you must have said something wrong at the office to be set guarding the scene," I preened, hoping that I was playing the reporter correctly. Usually, I was the one shielding people from reporters, not digging for information. It was quite fun to be playing the other side. I did my best to copy those reporters who had hounded us marketing types at Harcourt most. Janos immediately started covering his reputation, which meant he gave away a whole lot more than he meant to. This is why you hire professionals to do your digging—and your cover ups. We just notice so much more.

"Punishment? I'm not being punished, I'm out her to continue with the investigation. I was looking for evidence of the victim's involvement in the jewel trade when I came across you two great idiots." Janos reached for his handcuffs, but there wasn't anything he could arrest us for. Not that I was terribly familiar with Norwegian law, but I had a feeling that just standing around outside a crime scene, far, far away from everybody else wasn't going to get me into much trouble. Even my questions hadn't done anything wrong, as aggressive as they were. Even so, my wrists started tingling, recalling my earlier experience with manacles.

"The victim was involved in the jewel trade? By that I take it you mean he was involved in the *illegal* jewel trade," I said, scribbling down the information as though I were an actual reporter. "Was he a thief or a smuggler?"

Janos said another word that didn't translate. I smiled at Yolanda.

"You two have no business being out here," Janos said. "Go away, or I'll charge you with tampering with a crime scene."

"We haven't even stepped foot on your precious crime scene," I scoffed. I looked at the cabin and then at Janos and sighed. Out here, with nothing to get in the way, using the aggressive reporter technique was going to get us nowhere. Janos was stubborn; we needed someone more amenable. I scuffed my shoe against the ground. "Actually, our car broke down. Could we get a ride back to town?"

"And let you ask me questions the whole way back? Not a chance," Janos stuffed his hands into his pockets and gave me the, "you must think I'm an idiot, but I'm not" look.

"No questions? Gotcha. Nothing on the record, nothing published, no names, no nothing," I said. I even stuffed my little notebook away to prove my sincerity. Please, please let this work. Janos narrowed his eyes and looked between Yolanda and me. Yolanda smiled widely, showing off her teeth. He huffed.

"Fine. At least this way I'll be able to keep an eye on you," Janos said. He looked at the cabin. "I still have some work to do. So you two stand over there. And don't move." He pointed to a spot about three hundred feet away. We wouldn't be able to get close to the cabin without him noticing, and unless we wanted a ride to town, we wouldn't be running off.

I shrugged and walked over to wait. Yolanda followed me, the human-image moving with her. When we got far enough away from Janos, the image faded until I was looking at the troll. "No questions?" Yolanda asked. "How are we going to find anything if we can't ask questions?"

"I said none of it would be on-the-record, not that I wouldn't ask questions," I said.

"But we are not reporters. None of it would be on the record anyways," Yolanda frowned. "What is the record?"

"Ah, official. Written down. Able to be used in whatever material a journalist-type would print. Not taken in confidence," I explained. "We're not going to get in the way of his investigation. We just need to know more about Magnus, so that we can find someone who might know if he was, well, hanging around with any supernatural types."

"You think that his connection to Life was involved?"

"I think that someone went to a lot of trouble to kill this guy with a supernatural creature specific to the Order," I said. "If it didn't have anything to do with the balance, it must have had something to do with Life. And I doubt whoever it was just showed up and killed Magnus out of the blue. I'd be willing to bet that they stalked him for a while. Possibly just met the guy in passing and realised who he was later. And bam, pow, no more Magnus."

Yolanda eyed me warily. "You have a strange mind, Cal."

"Thanks," I said.

Janos stalked out of the cabin a few moments later, looking distinctly annoyed. He jerked his head in our direction and started walking off, presumably to the car. Yolanda and I followed. We met the detective at a tiny two door Fiat. There was barely room for one person, let alone two men and a troll.

I looked at Yolanda and she grumbled something under her breath. She sighed and pushed the passenger seat forwards, climbing into the back with a good deal of complaining. As she did so, her form seemed to shrink to become the human image that the amulet portrayed around Janos, not the superimposed image I had been seeing. Once she had climbed in the back seat, she looked completely human, even to me. I squinted and couldn't see past the image to the troll underneath.

Was that part of the amulet's power, or troll magic? Yolanda had said that rock trolls visited the mortal realms for salty foods—among other things—so surely they had some means of disguise. Either that or Death's powers were a whole lot cooler than I anticipated. I shivered.

I clambered into the passenger seat and Janos went to the driver's seat, scowling as he put the key in the ignition. "I take it your search was unsuccessful?" I said in as friendly a tone as I could muster.

"I thought we weren't going to have any questions," Janos snapped.

"I said nothing on the record. No names, nothing written down or published or anything. I'm just trying to figure out what happened to Magnus," I held up my hands peacefully.

"Magnus, huh?" Janos threw me a wolf's grin as he pulled onto the road. "I didn't realise you knew the victim."

"He showed up on a Google search. You know, social media and all that? It can be such a pain to get rid of unwanted pictures and profiles," I replied easily. And it was true. It was a whole lot more difficult than people realised to get information *off* of the internet than on it. Social media sites were data hounds and did their best never to let anything go. That was why governments wanted them, why newspapers trolled them, and why people like me were hired to manage them.

I just hadn't bothered searching the internet for Magnus. I should have, now that I thought about it.

Janos glowered at me and shifted the Fiat into third. "If you're so capable, you figure it out."

"I want to know what happened to him as much as you do," I said. "And you'd be surprised how few people post their murders on social media."

"Please, Detective," Yolanda said in a tone far more sympathetic than I could manage. "It matters a great deal."

Janos was silent for a moment, his fingers tapping on the steering wheel. Then he flicked a glance at me, "You two aren't reporters, are you?"

"Why would you think that?" My voice came out softer, sadder, than I expected. I looked out the window at the passing landscape. Rocks interspersed with green were slowly giving way to trees. Tall pines and the occasional bare-branched white birch.

Was it winter? I hadn't realised. Time must have moved differently during my transition. Did that mean I had been at this job more than a year, or just the few days that it felt like? Death had said that Elsewhere touched the mortal realms at specific points in time and space. Then, if so much time had passed, would these humans still be investigating Magnus' death? I took a deep breath and hoped that spring just came later to Norway than I had thought.

There were some things I wasn't prepared to deal with, yet.

"You care too much," Janos replied. "Reporters don't care about the truth of the matter. They care about a story. If the story is wrong, they'll issue a new story correcting the first."

I smiled with one side of my mouth. "All hail the internet."

"Indeed," Janos returned my half-smile with one of his own. "The way I see it, you're either cops like myself, or you've been hired by an independent, outside source."

"We're—" Yolanda started. I waved my hand at her to cut her off.

"We're just trying to figure out the truth. And we won't get in the way of the police, alright?" I said easily. Calmly. Hoping desperately that Janos would believe me and be willing to cooperate.

"I think it's a bit late for that statement," Janos said in a low voice. He looked at the rear-view mirror and fixed Yolanda in his sights. She shifted uncomfortably for a moment, but kept her mouth shut. She was finally doing as I told her. "You were about to tell me that you were hired by somebody, weren't you, ma'am?"

"No," Yolanda shook her head. I could see a hint of grey skin underneath her human visage. Hopefully all Janos saw was a slightly-nervous woman. "I was just going to say that we just want to know what happened to Magnus. It's a matter of some importance," she continued, easily returning Janos' look.

The detective scowled more and swerved to pass a car perhaps slightly more aggressively than was strictly necessary. "You two are involved in this up to your necks. I should take you in for questioning."

"You wouldn't find a whole lot," I said. Janos didn't deign to answer, and I had a feeling that whether we liked it or not, Yolanda and I were going to the police station.

Turns out, I was right. We drove into a town with a name I couldn't pronounce and went straight to the police station. The town was one of those big enough to act like an actual city, with different neighbour-hoods, industries, a decent night life, and the crime to go with it. As a result, the police station had a decent number of cars parked outside. It was big and boxy and modern Scandinavian style, which meant steel and wood and very clean lines. It also had all sorts of inter-esting technology.

Yolanda and I were passed through the metal detec-tors and body scanners and deemed clean. We were then paraded through a number of offices that looked very much like how I would expect a police station to look, only nicer. I was thankful that we hadn't been put into handcuffs, yet. We weren't under arrest, just being questioned for being very suspicious.

Detective Janos had no idea.

Yolanda and I were shoved into separate rooms

before we could say two words to one another. She gave me a panicked, wide-eyed look before the door closed behind her. I tried to convey confidence in my returning look, but I'm not sure I succeeded. If she started spouting a story about Life and Death, we were snookered. The door closed behind Yolanda and I was led to my own room. The space was small enough to be able to hold only a tiny table, two chairs, and the cameras in the corners. There was a small air vent on one wall, but there were no other exits. The walls were also boring and grey, and the carpet didn't even have a pattern. A person could die of boredom—or anxiety—in that room.

Janos didn't bother sitting down to interrogate me, first. He just threw me a smirk and closed the door with a click. I didn't hear it lock, but I doubted that I would be able to walk back through the office without being stopped by one of the many people there. A quiet but subtle way of keeping me where I was.

I sure hoped Death's amulets were going to provide us with a decent explanation for why we were really out by the cabin. Because I didn't have one.

I sat down in one of the chairs, and the waiting began. I waited. And waited. And waited some more. Since there wasn't anything to occupy my attention, I let my mind wander over the last few days. I sure had been killed a lot. Almost killed. Same thing. But really, what did I know about Magnus?

One: he was, actually, a jewel thief. Life loved him for it because it was some sort of weird way of fighting for her. She didn't make things easy on people, so those who fought against her were the ones she loved. And she had loved Magnus.

Two: he had been killed with an Ennedi Tiger. Whoever had done it had somehow managed to circumvent Death in the matter. I don't know how, but I imagine it had something to do with using Death-style powers without Death himself. The Ennedi Tiger was probably significant, but the one group of people who had ready access to the Tigers didn't do it. Who else could possibly have done it that way, then? Someone who worked with the Order, maybe? With but not a part of? I would have to ask Yolanda if that were even possible.

Three: upsetting the balance between Life and Death had not been the purpose of the murder. If it had been, then the Order of Silence would have been involved up to their eyebrows trying to stop it. But they were certain that there were no traitors and, given their proclivity towards torture-as-loyalty, I believed them. Unfortunately. There was another reason for killing Magnus. It had to be related to Life's devotion to him, or his being a thief. Maybe he stole from the wrong person. Yolanda had said that the supernatural crossed over to the mortal realms. So why couldn't Magnus have accidentally gotten involved in a crime ring led by a super-powered baddie? Maybe.

Some part of my mind told me that I should be soundly freaking out about the last few days instead of calmly rationalising. I mean, I worked for *Death*. I had seen wyverns and trolls and vampires. I had been almost killed. A lot. I had been almost tortured. I was way, way beyond my area of expertise.

That part of my mind was just about to start screaming, loudly, when Janos walked in.

I relaxed my shoulders and gave him a friendly smile. I hope it was friendly, at least. Detective Janos frowned and stepped aside. Another person, this one female, probably fifty, with the sort of look to her that told you she was made of iron, walked in with a packet of papers.

"We apologise for the inconvenience, Mr. Roberts," the woman said. Her voice sounded funny and I realised it was because the amulet wasn't translating. She was speaking in accented English. "We only received your passport and Interpol identification a few minutes ago. The embassy sent a courier as soon as they determined where you were."

Interpol, huh? And an embassy sending a courier? Just who exactly did she think I was?

"It's no problem, really," I said, assuring her with my best PR voice. I took the papers and flipped through them. There was a passport—American—as well as an Interpol badge, a form for sending lost property, and a letter certifying my need to work on the Magnus case. "No harm done, Ms…"

"Wilkerson. Chief Wilkerson," she replied, showing her teeth in a feral smile. It was probably meant to intimidate me into playing the docile investigator, only here to help. Unfortunately for Chief Wilkerson, I had been intimidated by things far more dangerous than she. Things even Yolanda was scared of.

"A pleasure." I extended my hand and she shook it stiffly. "Now, I know that it's getting rather late, but if you have a copy of the files thus far, then I'd love to look over them."

"Of course," Wilkerson jerked her head in a nod. "Detective, please get Inspector Roberts and his assistant the files."

"They're in Norwegian," Janos muttered in that same language. Wilkerson's eyes flashed.

"It's no problem," I said. "I can read them."

The two police officers exchanged a look and strode out of the room, Janos following his chief closely, while I strolled along behind them. Yolanda was already waiting for me, her face set in a scowl. I squinted to look through the image and saw that her troll-features were looking even more stony and grumpy than usual. For such a nice person, she really needed to learn how to smile more.

"Any problems?" I asked, doing my best to be gentle.

"They kept asking me questions. Twisting my words around so that no matter what I said, it was making me look like I was involved," Yolanda growled. The sound rumbled through the floor and I felt it in my feet. I put a hand on her arm, alarmed.

"They know we're not involved," I assured her. "We're just here to help the investigation along."

Yolanda shook her own packet of papers in understanding. The grumpy expression remained.

Janos handed us a disappointingly slim case file and walked off before I could even ask for a place to read it in peace. I sighed and found an empty conference room, ignoring the stares of all the people we passed. Whispers followed in our wake and Yolanda's expression soured further. I closed the door behind us with a definitive click and pulled out a chair. Yolanda followed suit, slouching. I started flipping through the file, reading as quickly as I could manage. It quickly became apparent that the human authorities knew even less than we did.

"Cause of death: disembowelling," I read out from the file. "No duh. Evidence at crime scene…nothing of significance to indicate a killer. Really! Here we go, known associates: Marcus Rousseau, import-export specialist, friend. Alice Nuberg, possible girlfriend. Criminal associates: unknown. Occupation: unknown, suspected thief. And that is pretty much the end of the file."

"We know he was a thief," Yolanda said helpfully. I pulled off my glasses and cleaned them on my shirt, stifling a yawn. "Maybe his girlfriend knows something."

"I'd be more willing to bet that the import-export guy, Rousseau, is involved," I said. "If that's not a code-name for smuggling, I really don't know what is. Besides, how many secrets do people keep from their significant others? A lot, going by the rate of divorce in the mortal realms."

Yolanda considered, tilting her head. The human

image wavered for a moment, her eyes flashing more yellow than green. "Those are the only people they know of? What if they don't know anything?"

I shrugged, closing the file. "I would say that something is better than nothing. I'd bet you all the salted snacks in the office that this Rousseau guy knows something. I mean, surely even the magical community here in the mortal realms needs to move things discreetly. Right?"

Yolanda nodded. "There are many things that can only be found in the mortal realms that the magical community wants. Salty foods. Jewels of certain qualities. Potion ingredients, like ground bone."

"Ground...bone?" I gulped. "Please tell me that's chicken bone."

"Oh, no!" Yolanda beamed. "Human bone. Very useful for many potions and charms. Adds extra... oomph? I think that's the word."

I took in a deep breath and closed my eyes. "You know, maybe there are some things you shouldn't tell me. Let's just focus on the job at hand, alright? We know two of Magnus' associates. Let's hope that the answers lie with them, or we'll have nothing. Rousseau first; he's my best guess."

"We go see him, then?" Yolanda pushed up from her seat at the table with inhuman eagerness. I glared at her, feeling the effects of everything that had happened that day. Also, it really was getting late. I didn't know the time difference between Elsewhere and Norway, but I was definitely jet-lagged.

"Tomorrow," I said, rising and gathering all the papers together. The passport and badge I shoved into a pocket. I slipped the file under my arm to be returned to Janos. "It's late. I've been bound and captured by the Order of Silence. I've been almost killed multiple times. I've travelled between worlds and gotten nowhere in the investigation. I'm tired."

Yolanda nodded. "I will find a brothel for the evening."

"Hotel," I said, pinching my nose. "It's a hotel, not a brothel."

"Oh."

"You really have the most frustrating blanks in your vocabulary," I told my assistant. Mostly, her lilting talk was fine, and she explained unfamiliar Elsewhere topics extremely well. But, really. "Where did you learn English?"

"A correspondence course!" Yolanda replied with a big grin, showing off her white teeth. "And the internet. I like watching videos."

"Of course you do. Come on, let's go find a hotel."

DROP DEAD

I slept as though I hadn't felt a bed for days. It was more than magical, which was saying something considering my life now. When I woke, the sun was streaming in the windows and things were looking a whole lot less horrible than they had the day before. Also, my phone was ringing.

Where in the world had I gotten a phone?

"Hello?" I answered groggily. Hearing nothing, I looked at the caller ID and saw an unfamiliar number, so I held the device to my ear again. "Hello?"

"Mr. Roberts," a sharp voice snapped at me through the phone. I sighed.

"Good morning, Chief Wilkerson," I said, sitting up. I half-expected to feel as badly as I had done when waking up in the hospital with Graveltoes peering at me. I was pleased, then, when the reality was that I felt more or less human. My wrists were a little sore, and the cuts that I had received at spear-point were stretching under their scabs, but on the whole, I felt pretty okay. "What can I do for you?"

"Detective Janos informed me that you had not provided any new insights into the case," Wilkerson said. "I would presume that Interpol has a reason for sending you here?"

"Yes, of course they do," I replied. At least, they would have done if I had actually been Interpol. I just had no intention of telling her the real reason why I was here or why I was interested in Magnus. "Though I was told to keep the number of people who had the details down as close to zero as possible."

"Well, I look forward to hearing your debrief as soon as you get in," Wilkerson snarled and hung up the phone. I sighed and threw the mobile to the bed. Then I shuffled over to take a shower, which was almost as magical as sleep. Clean and rested, I felt like an entirely new man.

I found Yolanda in the bar area of the hotel, where breakfast was being served in a buffet. She and I were some of the few people still working on breakfast. Apparently I had slept a whole lot later than intended, which didn't bother me in the slightest. Yolanda was happily munching away at eggs and bacon. Even as I sat down, my plate loaded with toast and some yoghurt, she shook about a tablespoon of salt onto her forkful of eggs and stuffed it into her mouth.

She was getting a few weird looks from the two other people in the room.

"You may want to lay off the salt until you can eat it

in peace," I suggested. Yolanda frowned, but put the salt down.

"Cal! Did you know they let you eat however much you want here?" she grinned. "This is my third serving!"

"That's kind of the point of an all-you-can-eat buffet," I said, ignoring the looks from our fellow diners. I poured some creamer into my coffee and took a sip. Oh, glory. The drink was heavenly, enough to send a jolt of pleasure through my veins. I hadn't had coffee in days, and my addiction was more than happy to be fed.

"What are we going to do today?" Yolanda asked around a mouthful of bacon.

"Chief Wilkerson is demanding that I bring her up to speed on the Interpol case," I said.

"But we are not...Interpol?"

"International Police. They deal in, well, international crimes," I explained. "The point is, we don't actually have an Interpol case to show her."

"What about the amulets?" Yolanda asked.

I took another caffeine-laden sip of coffee. "What about them?"

"They provide us with all the documents we need, no?" Yolanda cleared off her plate of the last of its food and sat back with a satisfied sigh.

"Are they that thorough? I mean, passports is one thing. A case is a whole different situa—" I gaped as Yolanda reached into a pocket and pulled out a full-sized Interpol case file. The file wasn't even creased. It was thick enough to suggest being significant and definitely official.

"Death is a powerful master," Yolanda said. That earned another strange look from the person sitting closest to us. She edged away with her chair.

"You may also want to keep mention of our mutual boss to a whisper," I said. "Such things tend to make the other humans uncomfortable."

Yolanda's eyes widened and she looked around the room as if noticing we weren't alone for the first time. We weren't holding a conversation that was loud enough for the others to overhear. My experience, though, is that people will start hearing you just as soon as you don't want them to do so. It's just a rule of life, and having met her, I could definitely believe she would do something like that.

Yolanda muttered an apology and sank into her chair a couple of inches. I finished off my toast and had a look at the case file. Most of it was an almost-exact replica of what the Norwegian file had said. There were a few points of information that they didn't know. Namely, that Magnus had definitely been a thief. His main work was in jewels and he was working with a fence in the area. The rest, though, was complete nonsense.

I pointed to the scribbles, "What is this?! We can't give this to Chief Wilkerson."

Yolanda glanced at the file and shrugged her massive shoulders. "That? It's just a suggesting."

I raised my eyebrows.

"A suggesting is a small spell. It just sort of lets people fill in the blanks. Nothing of importance, and if they want to repeat it to someone else, later, they'll have forgotten the details. But it's awfully useful for passing along false information," Yolanda explained.

"Uh-huh. So it's going to make Wilkerson believe that whatever is in this file is worth letting us poke around? That's a little disturbing. But also cool. I wish I'd had one of these back in my days with Harcourt. That would have made things so much easier with the old bat." I picked up the file again and stared at the squiggles. They didn't seem to do anything to me, but I was still impressed.

"Old...bat? Vampires do not turn into bats, they disappear into shadow...Oh, your old human master," Yolanda said, smiling.

I winced. "That's not quite how I would label my relationship with Old lady Harcourt. You know what? Maybe we should save that conversation for another time. When we're not in the middle of solving an impossible murder."

Yolanda nodded sagely, like she had a complete understanding of the universe. "It's not an impossible murder, since it happened."

"I meant that Death wasn't...you know what? Never mind." I took another sip of my coffee and Yolanda stared at the salt shaker longingly. After a moment or two of silence, she reached out and grabbed the folder, sifting through it.

"After we give her the file, then what?"

"Well, I really want to go talk to that Rousseau character," I said. "I have a feeling that he's involved in this up to his neck."

We finished breakfast—by which I mean I finished breakfast and Yolanda continued to stare longingly at the salt and the buffet. Then, we went off to drop the file off with Chief Wilkerson. She glared at me the whole time I was in her office, but promised not to share the information beyond her. I had a feeling that Janos would be surreptitiously handed the file sometime within the hour after we left. It wasn't my problem, though, so I didn't really care. If they wanted to investigate something way beyond their understanding, then I sympathised and also wanted to be far, far away when they did. So Yolanda and I rented a car and searched for Marcus Rousseau's import-export business with my mysterious new phone, happily leaving the police behind before they could assign someone to work with us.

We found Marcus Rousseau in one of those industrial warehouse office-parks, where the rent is cheap and your average person isn't going to wander in out of curiosity. There were a few planters around filled with a few tiny pine trees and holly bushes, which made the whole area seem even more desolate and sad than otherwise. It was like trying to dress up a dead man by putting on a bowtie.

The offices of Marcus Rousseau required that we be buzzed in, which was an encouraging sign for illegal activity, I thought. I leaned on the buzzer until the door clicked and smiled at Yolanda. "Let's see what Mr. Rousseau has to hide, shall we?"

I stepped in to find myself being glared at by a small, paunchy man with his arms crossed over his belly. He wore colourful clothes of very fine make and had an abundance of dark, well-trimmed hair. "Mr. Rousseau has nothing to hide," he said in something approximating a sneer. "As I'm sure you'll find out."

"Ah, Mr. Rousseau, I presume," I said, holding out my hand. The man's mouth tightened into a thin line and he didn't shake my hand.

"Who are you people? Cops?" he asked. I looked back at Yolanda, who was looming in the doorway, her human image looking almost as intimidating as her troll one. She shrugged.

"We represent another party," I said slowly, putting my hands in my pockets and taking a casual look around the offices. They were sparse, but well put together. I had half expected priceless antiques to be strewn about here and there. I suppose you don't make that sort of illegal business obvious, though. I needed to stop watching so many movies.

"What do you want?" Rousseau waddled over to a leather chair and sat down, the seat exhaling air in a whoosh. "If you're shipping, then I'll need all the proper forms and—"

"We're here about Magnus," Yolanda supplied. She moved away from the door and sat in one of the tiny chairs opposite Rousseau's desk. It creaked ominously under her weight. Rousseau let out a sigh, one of those that practically screams of great exasperation. He put his fingers to his temple and started massaging.

"What's he done now?" Rousseau asked wearily.

"Gone and gotten himself killed," I said. Rousseau blinked and leaned back in his chair. So he hadn't known Magnus was dead. That meant that either Rousseau's contacts from Elsewhere hadn't bothered to tell him, or that he wasn't involved. I hoped it was the former. I'd really love to be done with this investigation.

"Huh," Rousseau huffed out a bit of air. "Well. The man finally went off and messed with the wrong person."

"Why would you say that?" I asked, leaning forwards to show my very keen interest. Rousseau just gave me a look like I wasn't worth his time. "I take it that Magnus was often, ah, involved in trouble?"

"Like fish and water," Rousseau confirmed. "That man was always on one side of the law or the other. He drew cops and then promptly mucked the trail so they had to go somewhere else. I always knew he was going to get it, one of these days. He always swore he'd retire with millions."

"And were you ever involved in Magnus' escapades?" I asked carefully. Apparently I wasn't careful enough. Rousseau sat up straight and narrowed his eyes.

"Now, I thought you weren't cops," he said in a low voice.

"We're not," Yolanda assured him with a smile that was possibly too eager. I smothered a wince.

"Oh, then who's this other party you represent?" Rousseau asked. He reached into one of the drawers in the desk, his hand disappearing at the same time a scowl rose on his features and I knew that the polite conversation was over.

"We're trying to figure out who killed him," I said. "But you're going to claim to know nothing about that. And I'd believe you, if I hadn't known what killed him. So tell me, Rousseau, who controls your, ah, Elsewhere assets?"

Rousseau drew his brows together, "Sorry. My what?"

"You know, the things that you can't exactly store here in the mortal realms? Do you supply the vamps with their blood? Or perhaps some salt for the rock trolls? Maybe even send out whatever ritual elements the Order wants in the mortal realms for 'keeping the balance'."

"You're making no sense," Rousseau said. He pulled his hand out from the drawer and—you guessed it— was pointing a gun in my direction. "I suggest you take your babbling somewhere else, okay?"

"Yolanda, would you mind providing some visual aid?" I asked. She frowned and fumbled with the amulet around her neck.

"Do I have to?" she complained. "I hate it when they go and scream and shout and everything. Why can't you do it?"

"Because that requires he shoot me fatally," I countered. "And given the way his hands are shaking, I don't think that's going to happen."

Yolanda scowled. "Fine." She tore the amulet over her head and dropped it in my hand. "Happy?"

The human image flickered and went out and in its place was the troll. I was used to her by now, but Rousseau started screaming. He pushed backwards from his desk fast enough that the chair fell over. Rousseau scrabbled to a far corner and kept screaming. I handed the amulet back to Yolanda and she slipped it over her head faster than I could sneeze.

Rousseau stopped screaming and instead started to whimper. "I don't know who you are," he said, voice trembling. "Please don't hurt me."

"Hurt you?" Yolanda looked taken aback. "We are not here to hurt you."

"What do you want? Please don't kill me. I'll do whatever you say." Rousseau started to sob. Great heaving breaths tore through him and he pushed as far into his corner as possible.

I crouched down to look him straight in the eye, a little concerned at his reaction. "We just want to know what Magnus was into."

"Yes, alright!" Rousseau cried, starting to hiccough. "I smuggled some jewels for him. Nothing big, nothing notorious. Just the individual pieces that he couldn't get out of the country any other way. But I didn't ask where he got them and I never wanted to know where they ended up. That was all!"

I exchanged a glance with Yolanda. She was shifting her weight back and forth and clutching the amulet tightly. I stood up, pushing my glasses up my nose. "Ah, thank you for your time."

Rousseau let out a sound somewhere between relief and horror as Yolanda and I turned away. I had the feeling I was going to be hearing that sound for a while yet. We stepped into the sun and walked around the industrial park for a minute.

"Does everybody react that way to things from Elsewhere?" I asked, kicking a pebble.

Yolanda looked at her feet and shook her head. "No. Most of the immortal beings are predators. They create appealing images to lure their prey in. People only start screaming when it's us ugly creatures, or when the beautiful ones start to kill you."

"I'm sorry," I said quietly. "I didn't mean for that to happen. I never wanted you to...you know. I thought that he would have known and...sorry."

"Trolls are used to it," Yolanda replied just as quietly. "We are taught from a young age that we will never be beautiful. The only solution is to be strong, tough. Brutal. That's why you don't hear many good stories about trolls. Just the ones where they come in and tear things limb from limb."

"You're not like that," I said firmly, putting my hand on her arm.

"There is a reason why I work as a menial servant for Death," Yolanda said. "I cannot return to the Troll Kingdom. It would mean my death."

"He saved you," I murmured. Yolanda nodded. I chuckled a bit. "He seems to have a habit of doing that. Caught me just as I was going to be shot."

"I was about to be thrown off a cliff," Yolanda said, a trace of teasing in her voice. I responded with a half smile and kicked another pebble.

"You win."

"Huzzah," she said. "Now what?"

"Well, obviously Rousseau had no idea of any supernatural influences in Magnus' life. Or if he did, then they were doing a very good job at pretending to be human."

"Many predators can do that," Yolanda said. I scowled.

"Not helping. If Magnus had any supernatural, magical, Elsewhere involvement, then I would have sworn Rousseau would have been it. And it just doesn't make sense for him to have *no* involvement or connection to Elsewhere. How else would someone have known about his relationship with Life enough to have bothered to kill him? No, I think we need to have a chat with the girlfriend," I said. "Maybe she knew more about Magnus' life than the average partner."

"How do we find her?" Yolanda asked. I was about to answer with some snarky, 'I don't know' response when a car sped into the industrial park and stopped just before Rousseau's building. A woman stepped out and I nearly dropped my jaw to the ground in pure shock.

She was beautiful. Stunning. The sort to stop traffic

as she walked by, or cause accidents. Her skin was that pale shade that reminded you of milk, but was too creamy to be quite that dull. Her limbs were long and lithe and she had curves that spoke more of power and ancient glory than stick-thin models. Her red hair was bound back in some sort of messy bun that showed off a slender neck and classically sculpted features.

In short, this woman was almost too beautiful to believe. And I was pretty sure that the license plate of the car she was driving was the one registered to Alice Nuberg. Well that was convenient!

"Immortal beastie?" I asked Yolanda, pointing to the too-good-to-be-true woman. The troll let out a breath through her nose and nodded.

"Immortal beastie," she agreed.

"Right, then, let's go say hello to Magnus' girlfriend."

I broke into a jog and got to Alice Nuberg before she could open the door to Rousseau's. "Good morning, Ms. Nuberg. It is Ms. Nuberg, isn't it?"

Alice froze with preternatural stillness, her chocolate brown eyes taking me in. She probably realised I was human, because she smiled, laying on the charm a bit too thickly. "Yes? How can I help you this morning," she purred.

"Well, actually, we'd like to know exactly how you got involved with Magnus," I said. "And we'd really like to know who it was that you helped to kill him."

Alice's eyes burned away the chocolate brown into a poisonous green and she let out a shriek that could have shattered ear drums. It certainly shattered the glass of her car. Luckily for me, Yolanda had reactions fast enough to clamp her hands over my ears. She seemed unaffected by the noise, except to glare and snarl.

"Troll," Alice said, glaring sharply up at Yolanda, whose image flickered with the after effects of whatever that screech had been. My glasses, unfortunately, were cracked on both lenses, which didn't really help me see how badly the situation was deteriorating. I could see enough, though, to watch Alice take a step back. Some sort of shimmer appeared at her back and Alice curled her fingers into talons. Yolanda reached out and grabbed her arm before whatever was going to happen could happen.

"Do not shift, harpy," Yolanda barked. "We have questions."

"A harpy? Really? I thought those were supposed to be bird-woman-chicken things," I said. It was probably not the best time for that comment, all things considered.

"Insolent human!" Alice snapped, all trace of that former charm gone. "I will tear your limbs from their sockets and suck the marrow from your bones."

"Cheerful. Except, you have to kill me before that can happen," I said, spreading my hands in sarcastic apology. "Unfortunately, I'm having problems with that at the moment. So why don't we just have a nice, cozy chat, hmm? That way we won't have to introduce you to our boss, we get to figure out what really happened to Magnus, and you get to hang on to your life."

Alice sneered, somehow still inhumanly beautiful. That, more than the poison-coloured eyes or the glass-shattering screech, was disconcerting. "You cannot intimidate me into talking. You will never get the information you—aiieeeeee!"

Yolanda had twisted the harpy's arm back into a joint manipulation that you usually only saw in wrestling matches. Alice had to bend completely in half to relieve the pressure. As a result, she got a pretty good look at me when I stepped forwards and bared my teeth.

I was a human, sure. I didn't have any fancy magical powers or super-sharp canines. I couldn't sprout wings and I couldn't run at a bajillion miles an hour. But I could be very, very, annoyed.

"Did you know that all I've ever wanted to do was marketing? I was pretty good at it, too, until I got hired by Death," I said in a low voice. Alice whimpered at the mention of Death. "That went pretty well for about a day, until Life came storming in claiming that her hubby had killed Magnus, one of her favourite warriors. Death didn't do it—which I know that you know—and so I got saddled with the job of figuring out whodunnit. Why? Because I'm a human and I could go around poking my nose into other people's business without people expecting anything but ignorance and offence. Now, let me tell you something! Since then, I've been killed by an all-knowing Irishman, a very angry snake-thing, and I've been almost tortured by the House Vampyr and the Order of Silence. Obviously, I'm not dead. I'm just really tired of this investigation. I haven't slept properly since my not-death. So give me one good reason why I shouldn't just take out the last couple of days on you?"

Alice snarled, but I saw a spark of fear in her eyes. She twisted and tried her best to get out of Yolanda's grip. I didn't think Yolanda was holding the harpy hard enough to cause serious damage, but I could practically *hear* the joint snap out of place as Alice struggled against the hold.

The harpy screamed again, this time one of pain rather than destructive energy.

Her beautiful image slipped away entirely. I was left staring at a straggly-haired bird with the head and chest of a woman. She had wings that barely looked big enough to carry her in flight. Her feathers were matted with dried gore and dirt and she had claws bigger than my finger. Her eyes burned with rage. The harpy hurled herself at Yolanda as my assistant released her with an apologetic look. "You broke my wing!"

Yolanda yelped and held up a hand to cover her eyes. The harpy, though, only had the advantage for a second. Those claws did no more damage to Yolanda than had the vampire's spears. My assistant roared and that same shimmering the harpy had used to transform gathered around her. It was the battle magic, I realised, as Yolanda grew taller and put on more muscle. Her eyes lost their rational look and became pools of pure animalistic fury.

She lunged at the harpy, who screeched and tried to back pedal. But a bird with only one good wing can only move so quickly, especially with talons made for fighting, not running. Yolanda had her hand wrapped around Alice's throat before I could blink. I cried out to try and prevent the inevitable, but I was too slow.

The silvery streak that landed in the industrial park, sword flashing, wasn't too slow. Yolanda's arm suddenly spouted a good deal of deep green blood, the sword having cut easily through her thick skin. The troll roared and took a step back to face her new attacker, the wound already closing.

"Enough," Justice said, head bowed. The bandage around his eyes sported new spots of blood and he looked as though he hadn't slept in days. His hair was a mess, his clothes were rumpled and his sword arm sagged. "Do not hurt the harpy. She does not deserve this fate."

"Justice, thank you," I said, letting out a breath of relief. "If you hadn't shown up, our only lead on who killed Magnus would be dead. Not on purpose, mind you, but there's only so much you can do against a rampaging troll. While I work for Death, I doubt he would, you know, be helpful or pleased if that happened."

I took a step forwards, but Justice's sword flashed up to rest against my neck. He turned his blind-gaze to look at me and twisted his lips in a snarl. "Move no closer and I won't have to remove your head."

"Justice?" I asked, my breath coming out in a wheeze. "What's going on?"

"It is time for you to receive the fate of those who seek Justice," he said. The scary part wasn't that he was angry or eager or anything. He just stated that in a cold, detached voice. He meant to kill me.

Gulp.

KISS OF DEATH

*J*took a careful step backwards, hands held high. A few precious inches appeared between the tip of the sword and my neck. "Justice, what's going on? Why are you here?"

"You are interfering in the cause," Justice said softly, matter-of-factly. He kept his sword raised. "You would harm one who has no business in your inquiry, simply because you wish to pursue your 'investigation.'"

"Okay, first off, the whole harming thing was purely an accident," I said, looking pointedly at Yolanda. She nodded, the battle magic fading as she shrank down back to her normal size.

"Purely an accident," Yolanda parroted. "A reflexive action when someone attacks me."

"See?" I said, trying to smile encouragingly. I didn't know if Justice was truly blind or if he just wore that blindfold as a symbol of his position. I really hoped he could see that I wasn't a threat. "We just want to know about Alice's relationship to Magnus, and who she could have talked with that killed the guy. That's all."

Justice said nothing. As Yolanda shifted back to normal, I noticed that Alice had scurried away from the troll. Alice's beautiful human image was back and she cradled her broken arm with quiet whimpers. The harpy continued sidling away, taking shelter behind Justice.

I started moving towards Yolanda, who was also cradling her wounded arm, though it was healing rapidly. Justice slid forwards until his sword point rested on my chest once more. "Whoa! I didn't do anything!" I defended, backing up again.

"You thought to dispense justice when you had no right to do so," the aurai said. "It is my right to intervene."

"I just explained to you that we didn't do anything. The harm was unintentional and we apologise profusely. That doesn't mean we can let her go, but I swear we just want to ask questions," I said. Alice sneered at me, the expression somehow looking anything but ugly on her features.

"Look at you, human. Completely incapable of facing Justice. Incapable of figuring out the truth," Alice taunted. "He will protect me and you will have to go back to your master with *nothing.*"

"Justice, come on," I pleaded. The blind aurai's mouth drew down at the corners. He really did look terrible. The trembling in his sword arm was getting worse, too. "Look, you don't want to do this. I don't want to do this, there's no reason for violence. We can just sit and have a nice cup of coffee."

"Enough of your prevaricating!" Justice snarled. He lunged forwards and drove the sword into the space just below my collarbone and my right shoulder. I screamed and fell backwards, clutching the wound. Yolanda let out a cry and lunged in my direction, but Justice swiped the sword at her, too. She paused.

"I'm alright," I panted, though I was fairly certain that I wasn't. At least I wouldn't die from the wound. It didn't stop the hole from bleeding or pulsating with burning pain. I tried to stand and managed only to stagger to my knees. I decided that being stabbed with a sword was far worse than having my throat cut. "What was that for?" I gasped.

Justice was breathing heavily and his sword dragged on the ground. The muscle spasms were getting worse. He bared his teeth at me and took a step forwards. I managed to stand, though the world felt wobbly beneath my feet. I pressed my left hand against my shoulder. It quickly became warm with blood.

"Okay, seriously?" I gasped, my arm throbbing with each beat of my heart. I moved towards Justice, hoping that I could knock the sword from his grasp. He wasn't looking so well and I had a bit of an advantage. Well, okay, no. My only advantage was that I wouldn't die, that I could keep going. But I could still be hurt—obviously—and that could take me out of the fight really fast.

So I decided that I would be stupid and rushed

Justice. I had hoped that he wouldn't be expecting my attack, and he wasn't. But he was also an immortal being. That meant that even though Justice was looking rather the worse for wear, he dodged me easily enough. And then he swiped the edge of the sword along my back, cutting deep.

I let out a cry of pain and fell flat on my face, my wounded shoulder getting a good scraping on the gravel. My glasses fell off my face, the cracked lenses breaking even more. I grabbed them and shoved them back on my face with my good arm. The pain flared up enough to make me nearly black out. I ground my teeth and sat up, forcing the darkness back.

Yolanda hadn't waited to see if I was okay. She ran towards Justice, her feet pounding on the ground, her arms outstretched to beat him back. Justice dodged her charge as though she were nothing more than a raging bull. A mortal raging bull. He came to a halt about twenty feet away, his shoulders heaving with effort. Sweat was dripping down his brow readily and his shirt stuck to him. I thought I saw a faint spot of red on his own shoulder, but with all the other blood—most of it mine—it was hard to tell.

"Justice?" Alice asked cautiously. She danced forwards and ran her fingers over Justice's arm. The aurai flinched away a few steps. "What's wrong?" Alice asked, stepping closer. She pressed up against him in a very intimate fashion, running her hands over his sunken cheeks.

Justice roared and threw her off, jerking his sword

as he did so. Alice gasped and fell back, a long, thin line of blood cutting her from the top of one thigh to the opposite shoulder. I saw Justice stagger back as though he had been the one to take the blow. That didn't seem to stop him, because he just staggered forwards, his lips drawn back in a snarl. He raised the sword high above his head. Alice screamed in terror.

"No, wait!" I cried, moving as quickly as I could, the pain in my arm and back fuelling my desperation. I skidded to a halt just before Alice's prone form. Justice let out a wordless cry and drove his sword towards me.

"I've had enough!" he yelled. Getting killed by a knife hurts. A lot. Having someone slit your throat with a scalpel is marginally less painful, but equally as effective and startling. Getting killed by a sword, though, is like pouring burning gasoline through your veins. The other wounds Justice had dealt me didn't even register. The blade must have pierced my heart, because I had a couple of seconds of realising what had happened before the blackout took effect.

When I came to, Justice was ten feet away, leaning on his sword, drops of blood dripping from his mouth. Yolanda was crouched in front of Alice and me, her hands spread flat on the ground, like some massive guard dog. Justice cried out, fury lacing his voice. He tightened his grip on his sword.

Worse, though, than all of that was the fact that there was a small Fiat at the far end of the gravel lot.

Detective Janos was moving towards us, a tire iron raised as an improvised weapon. His eyes were wide and flashing. "What's going on here?" he asked, his voice sounding even more garbled than usual through the amulet. Yolanda let out a cry and started moving towards me.

"No," Detective Janos held up the tire iron. "Don't move! You are all going to be arrested, just as soon as backup arrives."

"Detective," I pleaded, "don't. You need to get back to your car. Call off the backup."

"You!" Janos said, fixing on me and ignoring the dangerous aurai with a sword. "You're the one who tricked my Chief into letting you into this investigation! You think I wouldn't notice that most of the file you gave her was *nonsense?*"

Great. I guess the amulet-made file wasn't foolproof. All things considered, it shouldn't have surprised me. It never rains, but it pours, after all.

"Look, Detective, I swear that I'm not trying to interfere in your investigation. You're dealing with things you can't understand," I said, holding up my right hand to stop him. I gasped and swallowed back another scream. My death wound had been healed, but my arm and back were still open wounds. Still bleeding.

"What...what's going on?" Janos asked uncertainly, looking closely at my wound.

"Human," Yolanda rumbled cautiously, "you would do well to leave this place."

Janos squinted at her, as though he could almost see through the troll's human image. He shook his head and raised the tire iron higher. Janos took a good look around. He saw Alice crouched on the ground, blood indicating where the shallow wound from the sword had been. He saw me leaning over her, my hand pressed to my shoulder and probably a big splotch of blood where Justice had stabbed me through the heart. Janos saw Yolanda standing some distance away, looking nervously between me and Justice. Then, Janos caught sight of Justice.

The aurai tightened his grip on his sword, teeth bared in a feral snarl. Justice's muscles were still shaking violently, and his white hair was plastered to his head. Most unnerving of all, though, was the fact that his blindfold developed crimson spots before our very eyes. The blindness of Justice was becoming tattered.

"Drop the sword!" Janos yelled, shifting his weight into a fighting stance. Justice hissed and raised his sword, though the effort looked as though it was too much. Janos took that as a definite threat, and rushed Justice.

"No!" Mine wasn't the only cry, but it was definitely the loudest. Yolanda was the closest to the human detective. She took one giant step and knocked the man out of the way. Janos flew about ten feet through the air before landing and skidding on the gravel. He groaned.

Justice's sword glanced harmlessly through the air where Janos had been.

"Why won't you just leave me alone?!" Justice

snarled. He took a step towards us and collapsed on the ground, his sword clattering a few inches away. "Just leave me alone."

"We didn't *do* anything, Justice," I said. I crawled around Yolanda and knelt in the gravel a few feet away from him. He turned his head towards me and twitched a hand in the direction of his sword, but it was pretty clear that he wasn't about to get up and continue fighting.

"Why are you doing this?" I asked. "I get protecting Alice, but why are you fighting us? You killed me, Justice. You were going to kill Janos. An innocent mortal."

"You are not dead," he panted. Even as I watched, the flesh on his face became grey and drawn and a few spots of blood appeared at his nostrils and ears.

"Why are you doing this?" I repeated. He shook his head weakly. A sound like a dying dog caught in his throat. "Please."

"Because I loved her," Justice murmured, red tears slipping out from under his bandage. I looked at Alice, whose face was caught in a look of horror and shock.

"You loved *her*," the harpy croaked. "But you said—"

"I know what I said!" Justice screamed. He banged a fist on the ground, but the motion was too weak to do more than raise a few bits of dust. "You were nothing more than a...a tool. To get me close to the mortal warrior."

I sat back on my heels. "*You* killed Magnus."

Justice turned his face away from me, apparently

unable to say the words. Alice let out a scream and lunged to attack the fallen aurai. Yolanda turned and held the harpy in place. Alice's broken arm was healing, but Yolanda put enough pressure on it to keep Alice still. She cried, though, beautiful silver tears falling down her face. Ironically, they made her look more human and more real to me.

Detective Janos sat up, "H-he killed Magnus?" The man groaned and tried to inch his way towards us. I ignored him, instead moving closer to Justice.

"Why?" I asked. "How?"

"You wouldn't understand, mortal," Justice said, his voice creaking. The bandage around his eyes grew darker as it soaked up the bloody tears. Whatever he had done was tearing him up inside.

"You...you said you loved her. It's Life, isn't it?" I said quietly. Justice's mouth tightened but he didn't say anything. I looked up at Yolanda and she gaped at me. "Life wouldn't love you back, though, because she only loves those who fight her. And you work with her."

"The devotion of those who oppose her is nothing compared to what I can give," Justice whispered. He started sobbing in earnest. "It hurts, Cal," he cried.

"I know," I said. I moved the last few feet towards him and put my hand on his shoulder. It was all I could do. I didn't know what was wrong and even if I did, I wasn't sure I could fix it. "Tell me about the Ennedi Tiger," I said, trying to take his attention away from the apparently inevitable.

"Mercy taught me about them," Justice gave a

slight laugh. "It was years ago, when we worked together on a case for the Order. They were beautiful and powerful and didn't care about Life or Death. Only purpose. They were like me...before I started to care."

"Caring isn't wrong," Yolanda said. She still held Alice, but her grip was relaxed and the harpy was doing little more than crying into Yolanda's arms. Janos had stopped moving closer in favour of gaping at us instead. "But you acted on that caring. You went against your purpose."

"I killed a man with no just cause," Justice said, his tone betraying his self-contempt. "I drew an innocent into my ploy. I eluded my own justice. And it's killing me."

I looked at Justice in horror, my stomach roiling with the realisation. He coughed and more blood flowed at his nose and the corners of his mouth. I saw the bloody splotch on his shoulder grow, the wound a mirror image of my own. Indeed, the wounds that he had inflicted on me, Alice, Yolanda, they were all there on his body, shimmering like the false images the amulets provided. But it was much worse than that. Apparently denying his purpose—going against what his very *being* stood for—was taking out far more from Justice than he meted out.

"Justice," I breathed, reaching out a hand. He curled his lips and looked away.

"Don't bother, Cal," he coughed. "I know exactly what you're thinking. Sympathy has no place here. I was in the wrong and I am paying the price. That is only just."

"But it is not merciful."

Mercy appeared as though she just walked through a screen. She had on the medieval-style gown and a sword in her hand. At her side stood Death, looking grimmer than usual. Shadows swirled around his form. Life was at Mercy's other side, her own expression barely containing hatred for the broken figure at her feet.

Alice let out a shrill cry and broke away from Yolanda, holding up her arms in futile defence. Yolanda bowed her head in trembling respect. Janos let out a strangled sound in the back of his throat that he quickly swallowed down. He recoiled back, probably doing his best to be unnoticed by these immensely powerful beings.

"Master," Yolanda said. Death paused at the troll's side. He let out a long breath. "We did as you asked," Yolanda continued, her voice shaking.

"Indeed," Death said. "And yet, I cannot help but wish that this had turned out a different way."

"You traitor," Life spat. She rushed forwards and delivered a kick to Justice's side. I flinched. The woman was still beautiful, still terrible, but she was also savage, too, and uncontrollable. At least, until Death stepped up to her side and put a hand on her shoulder with gentleness and grace.

"Enough, my dear," he said, voice low. Life let out an animalistic snarl and rounded on her husband.

"He has taken my beloved from me. He presumed to love me more! He will suffer for the insult," Life hissed.

"Magnus has passed out of your hands," Death replied firmly.

"But Justice is still in them," Life crooned, her eyes blazing—quite literally—with fervour. "And he will be dealt with accordingly."

Life reached for Justice, preparing to close her hand around his throat. "N-no!" Janos cried. He got to his feet and stumbled closer. Everyone, including Life and Death, froze and stared at the human detective. He was bleeding from a few scrapes his slide across the gravel had given him and he was covered in dust. But he just kept moving forwards.

"D-don't," Janos stopped just in front of Justice's dying form, putting himself between the sylph and the ancient powerful beings. "Don't kill him!"

"What is this?" Life asked, drawing her brows together. She looked at Death, "Is he another of yours?"

"No, my dear," Death said, his empty sockets focusing on Janos with great interest. "He is still yours."

"I'm not anybody's," Janos ground out. He clenched his fists at his side. "I don't know who you are, but you're going to leave this man be. He needs to be treated for his wounds, then brought to trial to face justice."

Life tossed back her head and let out a peal of laughter. The sound sent shivers down my spine and my heart started pounding faster in sheer excitement. My wound also started bleeding more heavily again, the throbbing pain returning with a vengeance. I clenched my jaw to keep from yelling at Life.

"Foolish mortal," she crooned, smiling at Janos. His face was flushed and he was obviously enthralled by Life's presence. I wasn't technically alive, and it was hard for me to shake that influence. The detective, by my guess, should have been on the ground at her feet, begging for her favour. He just stood his ground. Life spread her lips in pleasure. "You have strength, to fight me so. But you know not what you do. Stand aside."

"No," Janos barked, the word sounding as though it had been ripped from his throat. "This man is a murderer. He will face justice."

Life laughed again, this one cruel. "Do you not understand? He will not face justice. He *is* Justice. And he has failed. Who will deal with a failed Justice?"

Janos rocked back on his heels and looked uncertainly at the form on the ground. Justice was still bleeding from his nose and ears, and his blindfold was soaking up more of the blood from his eyes. The phantom wounds that the sylph had garnered were becoming more solid.

"Human," Death spoke, his tones gentle. "Your courage is admirable, but you must understand. He is dying. There is nothing to be done."

"Y-you can't know that!" Janos insisted. He shifted the tire iron in his grip, prepared to defend Justice.

"I can," Death said. "And I do."

"Listen to him, Detective," I said from where I crouched on the ground. My shoulder had stopped bleeding quite so heavily and I didn't feel like I was going to pass out from the pain. Janos flicked his gaze to me.

"I don't understand," Janos said softly.

"I know. But you must trust them," I said. I pushed myself to my feet and sucked in a breath. It took me a moment, but I managed to shuffle over to where Janos stood before Justice's prone form, valiantly defending something beyond his comprehension. I put my hand on Janos' shoulder. "They're not bound by your laws, in any case."

Janos looked at me uncertainly. He took Life and Death in again and nodded, though I could tell something in him broke. He stepped away from Justice. "You…you won't exact vengeance?" Janos asked.

Mercy stepped forwards, her expression showing some kindness. "No, human. They will show him only mercy. It is all that can be done, now."

"I could insist that he remain alive," Life hissed. "He did this in *my* name."

"No, wife," Death crouched down next to Justice and shifted him so that Justice was laying with his head cradled in Death's lap. "He did this because he loved you. There is a difference."

"He does not deserve my love," Life spat and strode off. Justice winced.

Death studied the wounded figure for a moment, shadows sparking around his head. "Do you know what you did?"

Justice let out a sob and turned to cling to Death

like a child. "I didn't mean to do it," he cried. "I was just so…it hurt so much."

"That is one of my wife's favourite attributes. It can be overwhelming and has undone many a stronger being than yourself," Death murmured, stroking Justice's hair back. I noticed that my boss was wearing gloves of dark leather. The leather wasn't as dark as his skin and it streaked the blood in Justice's hair. The aurai leaned into the touch, though. "You served me well, Justice, when I needed you. But you also failed me."

"I'm sorry," Justice breathed. Death nodded and continued stroking Justice's hair.

"I know. It is one of the hallmarks of being alive. Sometimes, you make mistakes. Have you learned from them?" Death asked. Justice nodded weakly. "Very well."

Justice turned to Mercy, who stood with her hands folded in front of her, head bowed. Her dark skin seemed to glisten with a power and I realised that this was what she was here for. She had come with Death to serve in an official capacity.

"Oh," I said quietly. I couldn't turn away, though. Justice didn't deserve to have me look away in shame. He was a murderer, yes. Part of me hated him for it. Another part of me understood. I wasn't sure which part scared me the most. Whichever it was, I had an eternity to get to know it.

"Please," Justice shook with crying, salty tears mixing with the bloody streaks on his cheek. Mercy took a step forwards, a small knife in her hand. It shone silver and seemed to hum with calm, peaceful energy. Justice turned to bury his head in Death's shirt. "Please, let it be you," he muttered, the sound muffled.

Death's hand paused. "Are you certain?"

"Please," Justice begged. The shadows surrounding Death grew. I shivered, a cold breeze blowing in the gravel lot.

"Very well," Death said. He reached to Justice's face again and slipped the blindfold from the aurai's eyes. I shuddered. Justice's eyes had been gouged out. The empty sockets were scarred and the remaining tissue was permanently pink. It looked like they'd been carved out with a key. Justice shivered as his empty eyes searched the area. The tiny muscles in his brows and around the eyes twitched, making the scar tissue jump. Death lay his gloved hand over Justice's eyes.

"May you find peace in what awaits beyond," Death said, voice firm. "May you remember and be remembered. And may you know that you chose this end."

Death leaned forwards until he was almost bent in half. His black skin reflected the light, until I was looking at nothing but a void. Then, Death lay his lips gently on Justice's head. A kiss.

Justice screamed in agony so great that, despite his weakness and his wounds, he bent backwards. His limbs jerked, the joints locked and the muscles spasming. The scream was torn from Justice until there was no air left. When the echo ran silent, Justice was dead. His body turned to ash in Death's arms.

OLD MAN DEATH

M y reaction to this mess was to fall backwards and practically collapse on the ground, my hands flying to my mouth to keep from screaming myself. Yolanda just lowered her head, her fists clenched tight. Janos threw up.

Life stared at the whole spectacle with her arms folded and her mouth drawn tight into a frown. "He was mine to deal with, husband," she snapped. Death rose and the last traces of ash were blown away.

It might have been just me, but the shadows that danced around his form were more lively, as if they revelled in the death they had caused. I swallowed and looked away from them. I had enough problems without my going mad.

"Justice was dying, wife," Death said calmly, removing the gloves from his hands. "He stood on the threshold between us. And he made a choice."

"He was *mine* to deal with," Life hissed. Death shook his head.

"He would have died in any case," my boss said. "There was nothing even you could do to stop that, not without destroying the balance and taking more power than is your right."

Life shuddered, a small moan of pleasure escaping her. "Be careful, husband, or you might give me ideas."

Mercy let out a strangled sound in the back of her throat, "Please, milady, you must consider the consequences of—"

Life swept out her hand, power rushing from her in a wave. Mercy let out a cry and was thrown backwards. She fell to the ground and stayed where she was, head bowed. "I know the consequences. Do not presume to preach to me, Grand Master."

"No," Mercy said in a low voice, one of complete obedience. Death let out a breath through his nose and said nothing. He walked over the gravel towards Janos, though he made no sound. Janos looked up at Death and flinched.

"Mortal human," Death mused. Life huffed and stalked over to stand beside her husband, her own feet crunching on the gravel as would be expected.

"He interfered," Life growled. She raised a hand and the skin on her fingers began to glow with power. Janos whimpered and scurried backwards. He didn't make it far. Death caught Life's hand and pressed a kiss to her knuckles.

"He was only fighting for what he believed, my dear," Death said.

"You're not...but you..." Janos spluttered.

"He is just as foolish as all the rest," Life said, lifting her chin. "He cannot even comprehend what it is we are and what we have done."

"Not everyone has as much experience with the world as those in Elsewhere," Death pointed out. Life frowned. "Even so, you would not kill the mortal who has done so much to stand up against you, not merely symbolically, but in actuality? You would not deliver him directly to me, would you? After what he has done today?"

Life paused, obviously considering Death's words. That alone was terrifying. But the smile she turned on Janos was even more so, filled as it was with the promise of everything a person could possibly want. "My husband has spoken true, mortal, which is a rare enough occurrence that I should take heed. You have fought against me this day. For this, you have earned my favour. Take my hand and I shall bestow on you *everything* you could desire."

"Don't!" I yelped, stumbling to my feet. Janos blinked, his hand already outstretched. He frowned and looked between Life, Death and myself. "It'll destroy you," I said desperately.

"But she said that I would have everything," Janos replied, his words muddled and almost slurring together.

"She's Life," I tried to explain. "Not just a powerful

being, but Life. *Think* about it! Life is cruel. She is unkind. She is deceitful. She is beautiful and wonderful and intoxicating and marvellous and full of amazing things, but she is not inherently good."

Life tossed her hair, the seductive scent reaching even me, and I was about fifteen feet away. It hit Janos like an actual wave of force. He staggered backwards a step, his eyes widening and his nostrils flaring. "Pah," she dismissed me with a casual wave of her hand. "He works for my husband. He is biased, dear mortal. He knows not what he says."

I looked at Death, desperate for interference. "I can do nothing, Cal," Death said. "It is the prerogative of mortals to chose their fate. If the young human detective chooses to embrace Life, then he is free to do so, no matter what the consequences may be."

I licked my suddenly-dry lips. Janos was reaching for Life again when I spoke, playing my last card, "Magnus was her last favoured mortal."

Janos froze. The grogginess faded from his expression and he looked at the spot where Justice had died. Then he looked at me and Death. He closed his eyes and took a deep breath, though I doubt it helped much.

"Who are you?" Janos asked, looking at me. "They are not human. Not of this world. But you…"

I kicked a piece of gravel. "Yeah. I'm human. About four days, maybe five ago, I was about to be shot. And then Death, there, offered me a job. I used to be a marketing agent. Had a good life, too. Now…I don't know."

Janos shook his head in disbelief. "How do you keep from going mad?"

I scoffed and shook my head, but I did smile. "With the things I've seen and done, I'm not sure I haven't already gone insane."

The Norwegian detective nodded. He straightened and looked at Life, who was watching all of this with the attention of a hunting cat. She licked her lips. "I will decline your offer," Janos said firmly. "I like things just the way they are."

Life's mouth split into a grin and she practically purred at Janos, "We shall have a good deal of fun, you and I."

She spun on her heel and vanished, leaving a vacuum of air in her place. Janos started coughing violently. Death waved his hand and the air pressure normalised, leaving Janos gasping for air. Death nodded formally to the detective. "I apologise for my wife. Know this, mortal. You have challenged her and fought her. And you have won. She will not make things easy for you in the future."

"C-can you, ah, make me forget?" Janos asked, barely louder than a whisper. The shadows around Death solidified for a brief moment, making him darker than the void he already was. "I...I don't know if I can, well, you know."

"I have done all I can," Death said and took a few steps away from Janos. He didn't look back at detective Janos, as though he were beneath Death's notice now that he had chosen his role in life. He kept walking until his shoulders lined up with mine. "I will see you at the office."

Then, Death vanished, too. Only he was polite enough to leave some air behind him. I raised my hand in a belated farewell. "See you later," I said into thin air. Janos coughed out a strangled sound.

"Cal," Yolanda said uncertainly, shifting her weight between her feet. "Should we do something about him?"

"Nah," I said, walking over to help Janos to his feet. He clasped my hand with a lot more surety than I had expected, given his last request. "I think he'll be alright."

"Alright?" Janos challenged. "The world I knew has been turned inside out. I just watched a man die by some means I cannot possibly explain. I was made an offer by, what, Life herself? And then that man, he was so dark, so...he would not let me forget." Janos shivered. He looked up at me, a sort of pleading in his eyes.

"I don't know if you really want to know everything," I murmured. "It's...it's not a happy story."

"Who was that man? The one who killed that Justice creature," Janos demanded. I hunched my shoulders and shook my head. "Please. Don't make me beg. I just want to understand."

I got that. Really. If I had just experienced something completely crazy, I would want to understand, too. I mean, geez, hadn't I been bombarding Yolanda with questions the entire time I had been in Elsewhere? I had questioned Fionn until he stuck knives in me—

and, if I'm being honest, afterwards, too. I had questioned the Order of Silence to the point that they were ready to torture me for challenging their beliefs. I still *had* questions I wanted the answers to. I hated not knowing things. But I also knew, in hindsight, that I would probably be a much happier man had I just kept my head down. I might have been alive, or better yet, going about my work without the knowledge that I wasn't really human anymore.

Being impossible to kill may have been sort of cool in the short run, and it had definitely served me well in this ridiculous investigation, but it also had given me a very firm understanding of pain. And—the more lasting problem—a very definite *fear* of pain, as well. I couldn't be killed. I didn't have the option of being released from pain. One day, someone like the Order of Silence could grab me and make me bleed and scream over and over and over again without end. I doubted that Death would come for me, to save me. That wasn't really what he did. I had already endured more in less than a week than I had in my entire life in the mortal realms.

There was also a point where being immune to Death would leave me feeling desensitised and less likely to care about life. I mean, wasn't that the whole point of being mortal? Wasn't that why Life loved Magnus rather than Justice?

I would give a whole lot to be able to go back and never have to worry about facing these demons. I also wouldn't give it up for the world.

"Alright," I said. "If you really want to know, then I'll tell you."

"I must know," Janos said. "If this is to be my reality, I must know."

So I told him.

I left out a few details, like my particular condition and most of my encounters with the creatures in Elsewhere trying to kill me. Janos stared blatantly at Yolanda as she revealed her troll shape. But he didn't burst out screaming like Rousseau had. And when I told Janos about Death, well, the man just nodded as though it made perfect sense. I explained about the Ennedi Tiger and Magnus' death. I explained about Life and Death and Mercy and Justice. And when I was done, Janos was pale and drawn.

"I...I would ask now to forget. I have received my answers. I don't need them any more," Janos rasped. He licked his dry lips and flicked his eyes between Yolanda and myself. "I just wanted to know the truth for a short time. Make me forget. I'll keep searching for Magnus' killer. I'll keep doing my job, but it will be *normal*. Not this, this insanity that you forced on me."

"I don't have the power to make you forget," I said. Janos curled his lip, eyes flashing with anger and desperation. "Yolanda?"

My assistant walked over and looked down at Janos with a small frown on her face. "I am sorry, human. Much of the time, your kind does not even take notice of our world. Or there is a rational explanation that they can supply in its place. I have no explanation that would make this nothing more than a bad dream."

"Please," Janos pleaded. "Isn't there someone you can call? Anybody?"

"I am sorry," Yolanda shook her head. "Perhaps in time, you will learn to adjust."

"You may never come across anything like this again," I tried to reassure Janos. He looked at me skeptically.

"I know this new, other world exists now. I know that Life is an unpredictable, potentially malevolent being and that Death will kill me with kindness. I do not think I can simply pretend it doesn't exist," Janos said. He put his hands in his pockets and scowled. It was darker than the scowl he had worn when we first met.

"Try not to jump at shadows," I said, pushing my glasses up my nose. It was all the comfort I had to offer. It wasn't enough.

"My colleagues will think I am insane," Janos frowned. "And I will have to explain to Chief Wilkerson about your sudden departure from the case. And then there is the issue of Magnus' murder. I cannot say that a...ah—"

"Aurai," Yolanda provided. Janos studied the ground, brows drawn together in bemusement.

"An aurai," he continued slowly, "I cannot say an aurai—whatever that is—murdered the thief."

I looked around the gravel lot, my eyes settling on Rousseau's warehouse. "I'll tell you what," I pointed to the warehouse. "You go in there and tell him that the people he just saw want him to tell you everything about Magnus."

Janos turned to consider the warehouse. "Rousseau? We did not think that he was involved. The man's records were clean and he is a coward, though he pretends otherwise. What did you do to him?"

"Nothing," I insisted. "He just didn't react to the fact that the supernatural, paranormal, magical world— whatever you want to call it—exists. He won't be giving you any problems, I guarantee that."

"And you? Will you be giving me any more problems?" Janos demanded, sounding more like an angry cop than a man whose world had turned upside down.

I didn't answer. Instead, I caught Yolanda's eye and tugged at my amulet. She nodded eagerly and we touched the pieces of metal. The world vanished into darkness, leaving Norway and Detective Janos behind. I had a feeling that he really would be alright.

BEYOND THE GRAVE

When Yolanda and I appeared in the office, I expected to be engulfed by a feeling of peace and the possibly mundane routine that was being a marketing agent. I expected to have my space be as calm as I remembered, with the chair exactly as I left it before leaving on this insane tour across Elsewhere. I had planned on having a shower and an enormous meal and perhaps not getting out of my pyjamas for a whole day.

What I did not plan on was walking into a war zone.

Mercy was standing in a defensive stance, one hand on the hilt of the knife at her belt, her expression twisted in anger—more expression, essentially, than I had seen from her since our meeting, even considering my ordeal with the Order of Silence. Standing opposite her was Agravaine.

He wore a pair of loose linen pants that belonged in

a Bruce Lee movie and a white t-shirt. His bad arm was held in a sling, but that didn't stop him from holding—I kid you not—a letter opener in the other. Agravaine was also looking angrier than anyone should really be in my office.

I wished I had a heavy duffle bag to drop obnoxiously on the floor, but I settled for, "Seriously?! Couldn't you two fight anywhere else besides my office?"

Mercy hissed and straightened. She lifted her chin in the air and looked at me pointedly. "I had come to ask you to take on the Order of Silence as a client, when this traitor almost assaulted me."

"I am not a traitor," Agravaine snarled, tightening his grip on the letter opener. "I left the Order of my own free will and I did not betray it in the process. I just exercised my right to a little piece of balance of my own without being tortured for it."

"You twisted everything the Order values and made it seem the demon before you left," Mercy snarled. "Our ranks are so unsettled by the happening that the fate of the entire Order is threatened."

"Hold up!" I snapped. Surprisingly, everyone quieted, waiting for me to continue. I took off my glasses and cleaned them, wincing at the cracks in the lenses. "First off, why in the world would the Order want me to market for them. After all, I'm the one that took Agravaine out of there."

Mercy mumbled something incoherent and stared at the ground.

"Sorry?" I asked, cupping my ear. "I missed that."

"She said that as you are a being of perfect balance, the Order feels that you are the only one who can rightfully advocate for their cause and paint a picture of balance for them," Yolanda chirped in brightly. "Also, you are the only marketing agent in Elsewhere, so who else would they go to?"

"Thanks," I muttered. Mercy huffed and stared harder at the floor. Her emotionless facade was completely gone, which either meant that this was a big deal to her or that she really, really hated me. Somehow, I didn't think that I was that big of a deal. "Look, Mercy, I know that you don't like me. And I don't imagine that's going to change, not after I had to go and find Justice…"

"He brought his fate upon himself," Mercy said cooly.

"Either way, you two were colleagues and I'm just a human, so that has to sting," I said. "But you can't honestly expect that I would take the Order of Silence on as a client? Not after what I saw there, and what they tried to do to me?"

"That is what I told her," Agravaine said. "She refused to leave, so I took it upon myself to make her."

"Oh, for crying out loud." I stomped over and snatched the letter opener out of Agravaine's hand. "There's no need for violence. Actually, I'm making it a rule. No one commits any form of violence in my office. Ever. Got it?"

"You refuse the Order, then," Mercy said, her grip on her knife relaxing slightly.

"I'm sorry for causing problems, but I don't like the Order. I can't do a good job of marketing if I don't even like my client. Not that I've liked all my clients, but there are some lines you can't cross," I said flatly, stabbing the letter opener into my pen holder. Yolanda squeaked. "What?" I growled.

"The letter opener goes next to the blotting paper," Yolanda whispered. Mercy let out a snarl of annoyance and stalked from the office, her dress swirling dramatically as she left. The door closed behind her with a slam. Yolanda grinned. "She will not be back anytime soon, I think. You showed her, Cal!"

"I thought she'd be pleased," I said. "I thought she hated me."

"She does," Yolanda assured me.

"Right. That makes about as much sense as everything else I've dealt with recently. Well, how about you go take the rest of the day off. And possibly tomorrow," I said. "I have a headache."

Yolanda nodded and left the office, though her exit was far less dramatic and far happier than Mercy's. I sank into my chair, bloody clothes, wounded shoulder, cut back and all. "Okay, Agravaine. What are you really doing here?"

The aurai sank into the chair across from my desk. "I am here to protect your interests."

"Nope, not buying it. Sorry," I said. "Look, I get that I helped you out back at the Order, but that's hardly a reason for you to hang around my office, protecting my interests or assets or whatever. You don't owe me anything. What are you really looking for?"

Agravaine studied the woodgrain on my desk intently, so I couldn't see his eyes when he said, "I have been disowned by my family."

I leaned back in the chair and nearly yelped when the slice across my back throbbed in protest. Now that the adrenaline of the fight and its aftermath was gone, my body was protesting its various hurts. Loudly.

"I'm sorry," I said. "Is it because you left the Order?"

"Yes, as much as the manner in which I left it," Agravaine murmured. "I was expected to rise within the ranks. Perhaps even work under Mercy or the Ancient One. It was my duty."

"And then I came along and you left the Order," I finished the explanation. "I didn't know it would end up that way. I never wanted you to be kicked out of your family. I just didn't want you to be tortured."

"No, you have nothing to be sorry for. The choice to leave the Order was mine. That it was done while I was being conditioned did not help my cause. My family felt my injuries were...deserved," Agravaine said. He turned to look out the window to the grey and silver lands beyond. "I disagreed. Now, I have nowhere to go."

"Well, you can stay here for a while," I said tentatively. I hadn't meant to get Agravaine into this trouble, but that didn't mean I wanted to live with him. I barely knew the guy. The fact was, though, that I was partly responsible for his predicament. And I had to do something about it.

"Actually, I was hoping you would give me a job," Agravaine said with a smile. It didn't quite reach his eyes. "I know you already have an assistant, but perhaps I could do footwork for you. Research."

"I don't...I mean...Do you even have the skills for marketing? Yolanda's good with computers, see," I tried to explain. The guy didn't need a place to stay, he needed a job? I had no idea whether or not I could even give him a job. What was my autonomy here? Would Death protest?

"I was trained only in the arts of war and balance," Agravaine said in a low voice. He pushed back from the desk, as though he was about to stand. "This was a bad idea."

"Now wait a minute. I was just getting an idea of your background," I protested. "I never said I wouldn't help you. You can be well, you'll be my secondary assistant at the moment. I'll get you trained and then you can take on clients of your own. After all, I am the only marketing agent in Elsewhere. I'm going to be swamped with work."

"I thought you worked for Death," the aurai said, though he was leaning forwards with a spark of excitement in his eyes.

"As you can see, I have people starting to pound down my door to get me to work for them." I waved my hand at the empty letterbox. "Though, Mercy did approach me. And the vampires kidnapped me for my services. All within my first week, no less."

"So I have a job?" Agravaine asked cautiously.

"Yes. I'll have to talk with Death about benefits and pay and all that, especially since I'm not actually sure about my own pay and benefits, but—"

"Thank you, Cal Thorpe!" Agravaine moved around the desk faster than I could blink and threw his good arm around my wounded shoulder. I let out a soft cry of pain. Agravaine didn't seem to notice. He just bounded towards the door and left, grinning.

"Ow," I wheezed, leaning back in my chair.

"You surprise me." Death appeared near the corner of my desk and I jumped up from the chair so fast, you'd have thought I was one of those supernatural types. The resulting scream was due to pain, not terror.

"Do you have to *sneak up* on a guy?" I demanded. "You scared the life out of me."

Death chuckled. "An interesting turn of phrase, given your current circumstances."

I scowled and sat back in the chair. "Ha ha, very funny. I surprise you in what way?"

"Young Agravaine there. You gave him a job," Death said.

"He got disowned by his family," I said. "It was probably my fault. It was the least I could do."

"The fact that you even consider it to be your fault is what surprises me," Death said. He held out a hand and the shadows congealed there into an image of a park. Actually it was the park where I had almost been killed. Creepy. "When we met, you were willing to take my deal purely out of self-interest. I had not expected you to care quite so much for those around you."

"Well, maybe you should have asked for a proper interview before you hired me," I grumbled.

"Much like you did with Agravaine?" Death asked. I sighed and my boss chuckled again, the sound eerily like a victory knell.

"Did you have a reason for being here?" I asked. "I mean, I did find the right guy, didn't I? Justice had... you know."

"Subverted my power? Yes. Though, I suppose it was my own fault for trusting him with it to begin with," Death said as if he were musing over a sandwich, not talking about murder and, well, death. "It is an interesting phenomenon, to be wrong about some-body. It happens infrequently because I so rarely interact with the living."

"Except for all of the people you've hired on here," I said. "Me—about to die. Agravaine lost his home. Yolanda was kicked out by the rock trolls for being too logical and happy. I bet Iggy has a tragic backstory. Mercy is afraid of showing how she feels. And Justice? What happened to his eyes?"

Death frowned. "You are entirely too perceptive, Calvin Montgomery Thorpe."

"Are we like rescue animals to you? Or is just that we're the ones Life rejected?" I asked, thoughts swirling in my head. "She actively defies you and yells at you and loves those who fight her. So why is she married to you?"

"Because Life and Death are a force made in balance," Death said, as if that explained everything.

"Or it's because you fight her. Very quietly, so that she doesn't even know it's happening sometimes," I said. Death stared at me, a wry smile tugging at his mouth. That was more than a little disconcerting, considering that he had no eyes with which to stare.

"I knew I picked rightly when I hired you," Death said. Then, he frowned again. "Though I did make a mistake in separating you from your life-force.

"You're here to kill me," I squeaked. I couldn't be killed by any other means except possibly Death himself. That probably made me too dangerous. I suddenly felt very light-headed. My mouth dried out and my heart pounded loudly in my ears.

"No," Death shook his head. "I am here to fix my mistake. I will make you merely immortal, not, ah...eternal."

"Oh," I breathed, letting out a sigh and leaning back in the chair. My muscles felt like water.

"What had happened was that I inadvertently replaced your life-force with your soul, which cannot be killed," Death said. "I had not anticipated the fact that humans require something on which to live. So I will fill you with an immortal life-force, taken from one recently dead."

"Justice," I said in a low, broken voice. My mind flew to Justice and the moments before his death.

Death had kissed him, had killed him. Had taken his life-force. And now he was, what, going to give that to me? I was partly responsible for Justice being dead in the first place. At least, it felt that way. I wasn't sure the guilt of having his life-force in me would do me any good.

"I have no other to give," Death said. "And I cannot have you running around as you are. There would be too many repercussions."

Before I could even think about it, Death reached out and touched me on my head. I screamed, the feeling of being pulled apart in all directions too much to bear in silence. My limbs were torn to pieces, to ash. I was blinded, my eyes gouged out. I could feel every wound Justice had ever endured. I could feel the pain he bore when he realised that he loved Life, and that she would never love him back. I felt the countless lives that Justice had taken on behalf of Death. I felt the influence wielded in defence of Life. I could feel the horror at having Magnus' blood on my hands—innocent blood. And the realisation that it was killing me. That Death, looming above me, had come to kill me.

And then, I began to heal. My limbs became solid once more. My eyes grew back. My shoulder healed and my back as well. Light bloomed before my eyes and my stomach roiled.

When I could breathe again without being nauseous or sick, I snapped back to reality. I was lying on the floor of my office, hardly able to move. Death was gone. I crawled my way up to my chair and saw a sticky note with flowing, unearthly handwriting tacked to the computer screen.

Cal, you now have one life to live. Live it well.

- Death

One life to live. All I could think was that it sure was going to be a strange one.

ACKNOWLEDGMENTS

If you asked how this book came about, I honestly couldn't tell you. I can tell you that it was a NaNoWriMo story, written during my year in Edinburgh. I can tell you that I didn't intend it to become a series, and certainly not on the scale that it is now planned to be. I can tell you that I had absolutely no plan for this book. But I can't tell you what it was that made me start writing about an unfortunate marketing agent that worked for Death.

If you don't mind, I'd like you to assume that it was something clever. It's just more fun that way.

As it is, this book and the characters in it have grown far beyond my control and will appear in many other books to come.

So I'd better thank some people for their help before things get too chaotic, though that should prove to be highly entertaining. First off, I'd like to thank my dad, who read the first iteration of this and said, "run with it." That, and our subsequent discussions of puns on Life, Death, Time, Space, and the like, have helped to make this book into what it is, and shaped the series.

I'd also like to thank Michael Evan for the editing and support. Let me just say, I warned you. It is not my fault if the characters take over.

Then there is Fay, who is such a wonderful cover designer. She took my initial shot-from-the-hip idea and created something beautiful. Then, she didn't complain once when I nixed that idea. Of course, she then went on to create something even more stunning. This goes to show why I rely on amazing people like her to actually do the covers.

Now, I thank you so very much for reading this book and I hope you feel inspired to go and cause some trouble. Cal Thorpe and co shall return in book two: Knowledge Aforethought, where I play with Time.

(Really, this series is basically me just going, "I couldn't help myself.")

ABOUT THE AUTHOR

E.G. Stone is an independent author who has been writing, creating and causing vast amounts of trouble since the age of six. Since then, E.G. has improved rather a lot in both the trouble-causing and writing and now spends her time writing fantasy and science fiction. When not writing, she is off musing about the workings of languages, both real and created, or drawing and sewing. E.G. reads voraciously, perhaps to the point of slight-insanity. Weird, nerdy, perhaps a little crazy, she is having a grand old time writing, reading, reviewing, interviewing, and, naturally, continuing her endeavours in causing trouble.